Lantern Road: Exile to the Stars
By John Argo

Salvage of original cover by A. L. Sirois

Clocktower Books, San Diego

Contents

Critics Raved about <u>Lantern Road</u>:

In <u>Lantern Road</u>, John Argo has created a richly-realized far-future world in which strange wonders are revealed as considerable suspense builds. The characters are interesting, and the plot moves well, but the real star here is the universe in which the events take place, especially the inhabited moon, Shur, with its complex star faring alien culture, reminiscent of Imperial Japan, but with strange complications--including multi-use fungi gardens and a third gender. Wolf's handling of detail is remarkable, creating a sense of a whole universe without bombarding the reader with unnecessary information. This is a world that fans of sprawling, far-future SF will enjoy immersing themselves in, reminiscent as it is of Dune and some of Gene Wolfe's work."

--Tim Pratt, Locus Online

"I very much enjoyed <u>Lantern Road</u>. From the start it took me through its twists and turns in a manner I never expected, but which fit perfectly. John Argo delivers a fascinating tale of tragic alien love, star travel, and an amazing gift from one love to another. For escaped slave Jory O'Call, the space port Kusi-O could be his only hope of survival, in spite of its impenetrability. But the bandit who approaches Jory on the road isn't what he seems to be. Then again, Jory discovers, neither is he... From a pampered court poet to high powered astropath, from escaped slave to free man, Jory O'Call's love of an alien female remained undimmed. Could the love of another alien, the Ramy-baba who even despised him, reach him across the stars?"

--Joe Murphy, author.

"Lantern Road is remarkable for several reasons. Most noticeably, perhaps, John Argo fully captures the richness and complexities of an alien world, focusing on its details and texture to the extent that you actually feel you're there. He also takes the time to portray and differentiate three or four different species and make them come alive, particularly when it comes to the trisexual Shurians and the poignant, bittersweet love story of Ramy, a Shurian, and Jory, a human. Indeed, the Shurians belong in the high creative company of Octavia E. Butler's Xenogenesis trilogy, in which humans and aliens mix their genes and get it on through the ooloi, a neuter third sex. Alien sex is seldom this good. What can I say? "Lantern Road" is a gripping story of the far future. It has high adventure, imminent danger, and a likeable hero. Plus, it leads to a surprising, fully satisfying ending that I guarantee you will never see coming."

--John Rosenman, author

"I had the pleasure of reading Lantern Road...and found it to be a very atmospheric reading experience. I was floored by many of the descriptive passages and conceits. Here are my thoughts, in more formal terms. John Argo 's Lantern Road is a sensuous and elaborate glimpse into a distant future--evoked, interestingly, by way of our storied past. Earth is a barely-remembered legend, man is a slave, and a unique species of alien (which includes an insect-like third sex...) dominates a faraway planet.

"But the story is accessible and immediate (rather than farfetched) because the writer, in lyrical, descriptive passages, has forged a civilization that evokes memories of the ancient Orient, with all of its imperial plotting and conspiracies. Our hero, Jory O'Call, is a slave, sold into a royal alien family by his poor parents. Visiting this protagonist's world is not unlike accompanying Marco Polo on his 'discovery' of the East. The story begins as Jory escapes onto a dangerous stretch of highway (think the Appian Way of

Rome, the Tokaido Road of Japan...) after a secret love affair is discovered.

"The author has given sufficient (and inventive) thought to alien politics, economy, history, and even courtly romance. Filled with descriptive passages and characters (like the bandit, Yafi) that evoke Akira Kurosawa films by way of Murasaki Shikibu's Genji, this is a texture-filled epic about man's legacy--and future--in a world more than 10,000 years (or *kjirz*...) hence.

"The blending of the historic and the futuristic, the familiar with the alien, makes for a lyrical, touching read, especially in the highly-charged, and sensual passages involving Jory and his star-crossed (literally...) lover, Lady Ramy. What remains most impressive about the novella is the author's observations about history and human nature, as well as the invention that has masterfully erected a world both similar and different from our own. So many of today's science fiction stories rely on technology, science or action to build their frisson, but the confidently written and very absorbing <u>Lantern Road</u> takes a different and welcome approach, allowing us to revel in sumptuous, compelling descriptions and details of an alien society, and man's place within it."

--**John K. Muir,** author/media critic
(SciFi Channel, Cinescape, Deep Outside SFFH, etc.)

Lantern Road: Exile to the Stars
by
John Argo
Empire of Time Series

Hardly anyone noticed a disheveled and breathless young man stumbling along the cobblestones of the Obayyo, the great imperial highway that ran in perpetual night around the island of Oba like a glowing ring of myriad lanterns.

For most of its length, the legendary Obayyo ran up into black mountains on one side, and down along the sea glittering in fog on the other side, always with a damp wind that was cold and cutting.

Anything could happen along the thousand *klix* of the Obayyo--so what was one more disturbance, one more running felon, one more pack of pursuing policemen in gleaming brown armor and elaborate helmets?

The Obayyo, or Lantern Road, crawled with an endless traffic of souls both human and Shurian, high born and low born, from lowly cargo bearers to traveling ladies and lords, knaves and thieves and murderers, clowns and fools and pilgrims, spies and merchants and priests.

Every ten klix was a police station manned by Shurians in brown armor with swords and shields. Every hundred klix the Obayyo passed through the gates and walls of an imperial district prefecture--a vast and grim fortress with dark towers and curving roofs. Dotting the mountainous countryside were villages where smoke curled from chimneys and wan light made tiny windows glow. Even less accessible were the mountain castles of local princes and lords, not to mention the distant forest haunts of robber barons. Life on Oba might center on the imperial palace, but all life circulated on the Obayyo.

The long ago sage had written:

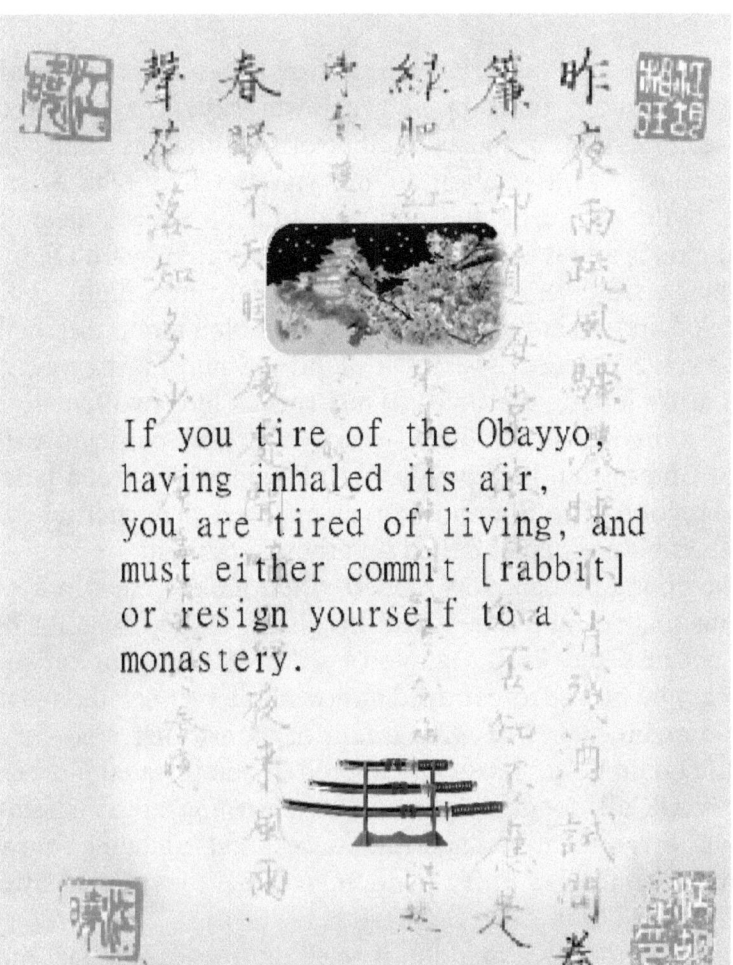

If you tire of the Obayyo,
having inhaled its air,
you are tired of living, and
must either commit [rabbit]
or resign yourself to a
monastery.

Shur was the single large moon of a gas giant that sent up a greenish luminous tinge in Shur's lower sky. The high road had never seen daylight because, as Shur orbited the gas giant, it turned synchronously with relation to the star, so that Oba Island was always twilit, while on the opposite side of Shur a steaming sea pushed clouds and winds with rain and humidity toward Oba.

Also visible in the sky, on this bustling night when the disheveled and breathless young man stumbled along the road, were Shur's twelve moons, the largest blood red and big as one's thumb held at arm's length, the smallest just specks like swollen silver-blue stars. The night sky was black in one direction, carpeted with stars like the lanterns on the Obayyo, but glowed milky green jade in the other direction. The Shurian natives called it their eternal daylight, while their human slaves called it perpetual twilight.

The young human, Jory O'Call, often looked back in a whirl of emotions that seemed timed with his sharp, ragged sobs for breath-- terror because the Lord Ramyon's soldiers were hot on his trail, regret that he had been betrayed and would never see the lady Ramy Ramyon again, worry at what might happen to her, and shock that one's life could be so drastically altered in one ill-fated moment.

Jory O'Call dodged right and left, earning angry shouts from hurrying cargo bearers, and the occasional glancing blow of a walking stick from a puffy gentleman. *Eya!* they called after him, 'filth!,' or *nah!*, 'rat!'

Jory's mind was a muddle of flashing images: the last moments of sweet enjoyment--then the door's breaking under ax blows, the retainers' shouts as they burst in waving swords, Ramy's screaming as she covered her face with trembling fists and realized her own end was near. Jory knew he would relive those moments forever, but nothing could bring her back. He would likewise remember, with dread, the looming third gender in Ramy's marriage, whom the Shurians called their baba, but whom humans distastefully called a wasp. Jory had caught a brief glimpse of Ramy's baba--a hulking copper-colored shape who was actually Ramy's sister--capable of the most terrible vengeance.

Something more had happened, Jory guessed as he tried to figure out why he was still free and on the run. His lungs made sawing sounds, and the thick, moist, plant-scented air scraped over his open mouth and throat. Not just the betrayal. Something more that caused the Lord Ramyon's retainers not to kill Jory and Ramy instantly. The retainers, as they were called, were petty nobles without land, who dwelt in a lord's castle and acted as officers for the ordinary Shurian soldiery, those being peasants and riffraff not far above the despised human slaves.

For some reason Lord Ramyon's men had let him escape. Were they expecting him to lead them somewhere? Ah! It came to him in a flash of insight. A conspiracy! They were always looking for a plot, a conspiracy, a plan to topple the lawful lord and replace him with some senior warrior. Oba was a closed society ruled with an iron fist, more by the cruel rigidity of its laws and customs than by a weak emperor or hundreds of petty quarreling warlords.

"Disunity is strength," said the long-ago sage.

That sage, however, lived centuries ago before the arrival of space travel.

In the foothills of the Oba Range, on the other side of the island from the Emperor's throne room, sprawled Kusi-O, the space port. Oba might be a backwater, but it had one extremely valuable commodity. Oba was a fungal treasure house. More than a million species of all sorts of fungi flourished in the hothouse atmosphere of the water world--some medicinal, others with manufacturing value, others for warfare, still others that glowed in colorfully. The lights on the Obayyo, carried in pretty paper lanterns slung on a pole over each journeyer's back, were fungal, bioluminescent.

Inevitably, despite Shur's isolation, visits had come from various interstellar trading organizations, bringing curiosity and commerce. That lure had been greater for the feudal lords than its perceived danger to their way of life. Meeting at the imperial palace a century ago, the lords had induced the emperor to sign a set of decrees establishing Kusi-O while limiting its effects on Oba. The space port would be surrounded by a high concrete wall. Inside was bathed in light, outside in the gloom of Oba. Aliens must never set foot on Oba proper under threat of decapitation. Shurians and humans must stay out of Kusi-O, or face a gruesome death.

The Raum Transport League and the Oban lords conducted commerce through a bureaucracy that filtered through the drum wall that surrounded Kusi-O, a tall concrete structure guarded on both sides. All through the gloomy night, gravless boats rose and descended between Kusi-O and RTL's orbiting starport. The pillar of bluish, hazy light beaming straight up guided Jory toward Kusi-O, though he feared how anyone's eyes could endure such brightness close up.

Tonight, there was no conspiracy, whatever Ramyon's men thought. Jory simply had no place else to run. Either way, he faced death. At least he had some place to run to, however briefly. How, he asked himself as his leather shoes began wearing out and the rough cobblestones pounded the bones in his feet, can I have come down to this? And what of Ramy? His heart ached for her, knowing that she was probably facing her father at his most terrifying.

Heart pounding, Jory jogged unsteadily along the Obayyo. Cargo-carriers, both Shurian and human, trudged by in pairs or quartets, with various sizes of fungiport urns hanging by knotted ropes from poles slung over the carriers' shoulders. Passing pilgrims and mountebanks blended with the vast majority of ordinary Shurian peasants hurrying to market. The Oba lowlands smelled tank-like of the sea.

Now one of the frequent fogs rolled in suddenly, making ghosts of passers-by. The fog smelled like sea weed. It blotted out the many wooden hawkers' stands on either side of the road. The many lanterns look like cotton glowing from within. Jory remembered delicate ancient Oba poems, of which he was a specialist. One liners. Two liners. Three liners. Each a sacred tradition practiced in the rice paper walled courts. To compose a successful three liner over cups of *sh'w* after dinner was to honor one's host beyond all measure. To house a poet, even if it were a human pedagogue, was to display ineffable social grace.

All gone now, finished forever, in one mad moment, Jory thought. His rear hurt from a tiny cut where he'd barely escaped a cutting weapon, as he jumped through a window on the high castle ramparts just hours ago. He could almost feel the prick of the first sword point in his back as Ramyon's soldiers caught up with him, or the Obayyo police in the brown and brass armor with elk-horn helmets. He could foresee the way he would tumble on the cobblestones, captured in a hard fishing net, and dragged behind a horse to the castle, where his head would wind up on one parapet, his torso on another with his mingled arms, legs, and inner organs suspended in a net basket for all the world to see. The long ago sage had said: "When an Shurian does something wrong, that is a crime. When a human does something wrong, that is a crime. When Shurian and human do things wrong together, that is an abomination."

Jory heard a voice at his side--a rough man's voice, human-- "That's quite a pair of horns you have there, *Nah*."

Startled, then angry, Jory veered from his course and nearly bumped into an elderly baba lugging heavy sacks under each arm. She hissed at him, exposing the long, thin tongue-spike that was her sex organ. Her normally mud-brown eyes flared with a dim greenish glow, a sign that she was high on a fungal opiate that many peasants used to dull their existence.

Jory dodged past her. The speaker was a very thin human man of medium height, extremely thin. He must not have shaved in a week, for a gray-brown stubble populated the pasty wrinkles of his face. His hard eyes suggested mingled climates of dishonesty, greed, cruelty, and occasional flashes of kindness or mercy in the "inner land," as the Shurians called it. "Go away, bandit. I have no time for you."

The man, who wore a plain hempen cloak and hood, and carried a thin wooden walking stick, fell in beside him. "Oho! The fugitive is gutsy!"

Jory stopped. He reached over, bunched his fist in the other's cloak at the neck, and pulled him close. "I don't have time for this. What do you know about me? What do you want?"

The man's strength was surprising, despite his light frame. He captured Jory's hands in his and twisted them against his chest, while pressing the point of his stick against Jory's ribs. Jory, however, had studied with the castle retainers. He had traded lines of poetry for the calligraphy of parries and chops. He had learned from the bored and sometimes laughing warriors the alternative tensions between the soft, circular movements of the go and the harsh, angular movements of the ko schools of manual combat.

In an instant, Jory stepped behind the man while his hands were still trapped under the man's back-turned wrists. Jory dropped into a spread-leg stance that made his center of gravity lower than the other's. By leaning forward and subtly shifting his hip, Jory threw the man, and the man landed with a thud on his side. Jory stepped on the stick so it couldn't be lifted against him. "What other tricks can you show me, you oaf, before I make you into fish food?"

"All right! Let go!"

"You have one instant to tell me why I should. Or I should break your neck and move on." Jory was still panting from his run, and he looked nervously from side to side.

"I can save you, Master!" To call a human Master was mockery, but this bandit was sincerely trying to curry favor.

"I don't believe you."

"Let's head for Kusi-O."

"You must be crazy." But that was where he was headed anyway, to die, impaled on the space port's locked and steel-studded wooden gate. Driven by the need to move on, Jory let him up.

The man gathered his stick and fell in again. "I'm sorry, Master, I'm a simple sort, and my mouth gets me in trouble."

"You are a fool, and here I am beside you."

"Who is the greater fool, Master?"

"You have a point there." Jory could close his eyes and still inhale the fragrance of Ramy's berry perfume. He remembered the silky feel of her skin, and the aroused pungency of her tongue.

The man whispered: "My name is Yafi. I come from Anamo, outside Kusi-O."

A territory of ruffians, Jory thought, known everywhere on the island of Oba. Kusi-O, interstice between Oba and the universe. Sluice of evil.

"There is a price on your head, Master. Lord Ramyon has sent runners in both directions on the Great Road."

"Thank you for information I already know."

"I must ask a favor of you before I go any further with you, Master. Will you stop a moment?"

"Oh what is this!" Jory said, stomping his feet impatiently, while Yafi felt around Jory's head with nimble fingertips until he found the hard round plates at each temple. "Ah! Just as the gate mouse said. You have the unborn horns."

Jory shoved him away and resumed a fast walk. "I have always had them."

Yafi walked beside him, pressing against his side, so that Jory had to keep pushing him away. "Master, it is something that makes you desirable to somebody in the Kusi-O and may save your life."

"You are delivering me to the Kusi-O?"

"Only by your leave, Master."

"You risk your life by even speaking with me. The price must be great."

Yafi's smile was sly, his eyes closing briefly in cagey admission. "It is so. But I cannot drag you there against your will."

Jory calculated desperately. What kind of trap was this? "Who wants these unborn horns of mine, and why?" He rubbed his hands on the rough, ringed surfaces that occupied a half a palm's width circle before and slightly above each ear. They were like hair or fingernails. It was part of him, but without feeling. A sharp blow to the head during stick practice with the retainers had once made the cuticle around these giant thumbnail things bleed, but other than that they were simply always there and he hardly ever thought of them, anymore than he thought of his toenails. Human girls had made fun of him and, though he'd bedded some over the kjirs, refused to stay with him.

Could this be a ruse? Was Yafi a procurer for some criminal element? But they would want young boys, not men nearing 240 *mendz*--the tool by which human women subversively kept track of time during the centuries since humans had been reduced from conquerors to being slaves at best, or hunted and killed throughout the Galaxy--a span, as legend had it, of over 10,000 mendz by now.

Yafi replied: "Both things are secrets I don't know and therefore regretfully cannot reveal, though you should esteem my honesty."

"All right, I'll grant you that much."

"I was a teacher before I fell on hard times."

"A teacher of what?"

"History."

Jory's interest perked. He remembered a night of murder and riot, but also of high discussion and noble words. "Do you know anything of a certain society, ruffian?"

Yafi nodded slowly, breaking into a triumphant grin. "The Twelve Moon Society, perhaps?"

"Yes!" Jory almost yelled and grabbed the man by the shoulder. "Does it still exist?"

"Ohh...there are rumors. Then again, it may be swamp gas to assert such things. Or else, if true, they would not advertise, not after their heads decorated the Obayyo from Ramyo to Menshu, your uncle's among them."

"Stop riddling me, you fool, or I'll hoist you." Why was the man so infuriatingly vague?

Yafi spoke soberly: "There are beings from many worlds in the Kusi-O. I have seen them. Great hairy beings who captain starships. They come down with their boats to collect cargo. Sometimes they want something special. They don't say why. It is deadly dangerous for a human to be in Kusi-O, and I do not ask questions. I keep my mouth shut. And so will you?"

"How will we get in?"

"Yes, I will be by your side. How we get in is for those who specialize in that thing, who can hoodwink the emperor's road police and the constables in Anamo, not to mention the Fril cops on the other side."

Jory had only seen Fril one time--they were almost never permitted outside Kusi-O--and that had been at the imperial court. Fril were humanoid, bipedal, two-armed, but they were more snake. They had fine shimmering scales all over their bodies. Their body color was silver, stippled with small and large yellow scales. Jory remembered admiring their bright, almost faint coloring as they stood to one side in long transparent robes while Lord Ramyon made audience with the emperor. The Fril, who were the officials and doers of all things in Kusi-O, came from another planet in this system. They were peaceful and honest, and fiercely devoted to their gods, which kept them pure. They were ideal keepers for the sluice of evil that could easily poison the Oba society, which had swallowed Kusi-O into its belly as a Shurian swallowed the proverbial mushroom. This saying referred to eating a tiny mushroom of one kind, thinking it to be tasty and filling, only to discover one had swallowed its sister type, which contained a poison so deadly that feudal retainers tipped their arrow heads and sword blades with it. By the time the eater realized the mistake, one was half dead. Many a disgraced official had used that very mushroom rather than slice his entrails out in duello. The Oba feudal system trusted the Fril to maintain an unchanging status quo. The Fril cops, if they caught a human or a Shurian inside Kusi-O, would turn them over to the Obayyo police at the Anamo gate inside the great concrete drum wall.

The gate was called Return of Property to Rightful Owner.

Just hours ago, Jory had waited on the high walls above the women's quarters at Castle Ramyon, among flowing chrysanthemum banners.

The area around Castle Ramyon always had a certain unique smell, a floral-like scent of the tywix fungus. In fact it was the time of the tywix festival in the villages around Ramyon, for the fabled mushroom was in the beginning of its annual throe season, when it had soaked up just enough water to suddenly proliferate across the landscape in a myriad of dimly glowing saucer shapes big as a man's hand. And they had a certain smell--sweet as honey, musky as river flowers, mild as oats. They were prized among the finest of Oba's fungal wealth, and ships carried them all over the local galaxy.

The night always had a certain charm and magic, Jory O'Call thought as he leaned on the parapets high above Lord Ramyon's castle, which itself overlooked a series of wildly plunging gorges above a forest, a lake, a small town, and, of course, the flow of lights five klix away on the Obayyo.

While he waited for the baba to leave Lady Ramy's suite and retire to her own unknowable dark hole, Jory must have patience and wait. Ramy would be waiting for him, eager to share the latest poem, the silliest joke or gossip about the castle, and, of late, embraces that led to ever greater risk.

Jory had grown up at the castle and knew the limits. He could get away with things no other human could. He was at the Lord Ramyon's pleasure, though the old warrior would have little speech with him. As long as Jory guided Ramyon's youngest and favorite daughter Ramy in matters of ancient Oba poetry and song, and did not transgress too badly, Jory was tolerated with a certain wink, a laugh, the patient air with which one treated a pet. After all, to see a human dressed in Oba court robes--moss-green silk coat, broad mint-white silk sash and camiss, ankle-length moss-green kilt, sturdy wooden sandals--was like seeing an animal dressed like a person. Ramyon had reason to be complacent. He was getting older. All three of his sons were married and in the field, keeping Ramyon's enemies at bay and the retainers in line. His house babas were strong in commerce and dark arts. All four of his daughters were married off and the matter of dowries finished. Only his youngest, Ramy, lived at home half the time, the other half at Dumonhi when her husband was home from the wars. Lord Ramyon, still fierce looking with his black robes and swords, could stride about the palace gardens picking moon roses, listening to Ramy's tinkling voice singsong ancient riddles and poems, and smiling at Jory as if the latter were a lap dog.

As a human, Jory was wallpaper, as the retainers said. Early in his childhood, Jory had been chosen for his talents at art and music to become a child pedagogue to the Ramyon children. Whatever their lowly status, the humans could sometimes produce prodigious talent. Every generation, a few humans made their way to some of the larger castles as prodigies, as wonders, as teachers, as oddities who could singsong Shurian epics and short poems with the deeper, stronger voices of humans. Likewise, a few bull-strong human men always found their way into each warlord's army. It was said that the robber barons at the far haunted reaches had more than one human among their gangs.

The Shurians took human children early, on the theory that they could be totally domesticated and would not bring any hostile ideas, such as stabbing the lord in his bed or throwing his children off a high wall--things that had happened in previous centuries, and were hideously punished, with entire human villages razed, and rows of chopped off heads strung for klix along the Obayyo as a warning to those humans carrying cargo on their shoulders.

But Jory carried in him an ember of pride, a spark of rebellion. When Jory was a little boy of about 3, his uncle had taken him to a meeting of the Twelve Moon Society. That was a forbidden group of

Shurian and human thinkers who schemed to liberate Oba from the warlords and give humans equality under the law. Jory had not fully understood the lofty words spoken around a warm fire in a dark underground warehouse while some 20 shadowy figures clapped and nodded assent. But he remembered the feeling he'd had, the infectious sense of freedom, the exhilaration of strutting about and speaking one's mind, even though he experienced those things through the mouths and animated expressions of others. Toward the end of the meeting there had been sudden chaos--the fire put out, smoke filling the room, men whispering in panic, feet thrashing this way and that, while Lord Ramyon's men beat the doors down with iron axes and tramped in waving their swords. His uncle had half dragged, half carried Jory to a window and handed him out to a passing cargo woman, a human who spirited him into the woods and then into a mountain hideout. When Jory was returned to his parents days later, he'd seen the rows of staves in the human settlement, in the main square. The men's eyes were gone, birds were busy about their lips, and their skin had turned black, but Jory could still recognize his uncle. His mother had let him see, as a warning, but briefly, before yanking him away. Up on the Obayyo, another row of heads on staves--the Shurian element of the Twelve Moon Society. The Lord Ramyon must have been satisfied that his informers had rooted out the entire nest, and his torturers put their skills to good use.

Jory had gone to the House of Ramyon at age 7 with a little human girl named Xinda who was said by the babas to possess a healing touch. Xinda had first come to the castle officials' notice because of her unusual hair and skin. She was that very rare human who had carrot-red hair, pale skin, and lots of orange freckles. That alone made her an oddity worth showing at the castle.

However, Xinda was said to have sickened a baba through witchcraft. kjirs later, Jory heard she had had her eyes put out by the castle babas one night, and the unfortunate girl had been sent out a back gate after midnight to the arms of her terrified parents. At the moment all he knew was that in the morning, when he woke up, her bed was stripped and her things were missing. She was gone, and nobody would talk about her. Life on Oba was hard, even cruel, but the Shurians rarely went out of their way to be cruel. They could be serene or cruel, because their laws and customs were unbending, and their warlords were desperate to keep all foreign customs out, even the evil spirit natural to humans.

Jory had been terrified of the dark, groaning castle with its blackened stone exterior and its whispering, creaking wooden corridors of which there seemed to be klix. Jory had been terrified to live among aliens who bred in three genders--the male warrior who was lord of his house; the baba, who was egg bearer, birth mother, and nurturer, and ran much of society to boot; and the female, who was sex object to both other genders, and egg source.

The Shurian males and females were very humanlike, while the babas struck little Jory as nightmare figures. The males and females had pale, almost translucent outer skin that covered a milky inner skin. Older men and women had visible blue or black veins just under the milky skin. Both genders tended to have a fuzzy globe of reddish-gold head hair like cotton candy. Because they were nocturnal, they had eyes half again as large as human eyes to gather light. Other than that, they might have passed for humans--although the very thought might have turned their stomachs. Some of the finer ladies, Jory found, were rather slender and attractive. Especially Ramy.

The babas were the horror of Jory's childhood, and he often ran away to his parents' house. Later, he would discover his parents, though they loved him, had accepted a handsome stipend for their son's services at the court. They always returned him, and he began to hate them. Later he just felt distant to them--he was court-educated, while they were ignorant laborers who could not read or write, and who had never left their village. Jory, by contrast, had traveled much of the Obayyo with Lord Ramyon's entourage, once even visiting the imperial palace. Jory had been 9 and had slept through large parts of that brief visit during which Ramyon had pledged obeisance while receiving the emperor's vow of eternal favor. Like so many things on Oba that were the opposite of what they seemed, this was a fiction, Jory would eventually learn, in which Lord Ramyon took 1,200 of his warriors and threatened to depose the emperor and murder his family if anything happened to the status quo. Hundreds of high lords did the same thing in revolving order.

As he grew up at court, Jory found that the dark, shadowy babas went out of their way to tame his fear. They were larger than the males and human-like females. They wore obscuring gowns over their round, bloated bodies. They moved cumbersomely like boats, on their swollen and aching feet. More than once, child Jory had nightmares in which babas with many arms chased him, like insects, though in reality each only had two very human-like pudgy arms with small hands. Their skin was dark, like a beetle's carapace, but soft as Jory's own. Their features were not as crisp and clear, or to Jory's eyes human-like, as the other Shurians'. Over the kjirs, he got used to them. They did him favors, though babas rarely spoke, and communicated in glances and signs; or had their female sisters communicate for them, which was more often.

As he grew up, Jory developed a bond with his mistress, Lady Ramy. She as tall as he, with fine milky skin. Her skin was so full of microscopic healthy young capillaries that in places, in a certain light, parts of her had a faint bluish tinge. Her hair was a full ball of tawny fuzz, always fluffed out.

Her tongue was deep blue, and twice as long as Jory's. As children, they had giggled and pulled each other's tongues. No matter how he tried, he could not stick his out as far as she could hers. Later they learned that sticking the tongue out was a raw sexual invitation among Shurians, and they never played that game again. Not until recently.

Ramy's face was well-shaped and as pretty as any human girl's, though by Shurian standards she was considered average. Shurians had a higher regard for a female whose face was slitty like an insect's.

Nobody, not even Ramy and Jory, ever suspected what would develop between the two. Like a kitten and a puppy, they romped and played innocently, laughing and wearing themselves out so they slept soundly after Story. For kjirs, until Jory began his own natural changes, the two slept together in the same bed in the women's quarters, under the watchful eyes of Ramy's father's old baba. Ramy's own baba slept in the mothers' quarters, though Ramy often went there to sleep with her. Then Jory slept alone. He wouldn't go near the babas' place, which was in a separate round tower of the castle, and had few windows. It had a coppery glow inside, and smelled somehow faintly of honey and ammonia.

Between the Ramyon family--the retainers and their families, the soldiers whose families lived outside the walls, and the servants and slaves--some 500 persons lived in Castle Ramyon. In those close quarters, Jory could not help but learn the intimate details of Shurian reproduction. Although the men were often away fighting wars, it was their duty to come live as husbands for at least a few months of each kjir. Usually, that was in the Lissom Season, when Shur was inclined slightly more toward its star, and the gas giant glowed more aqua than usual, and spirits were said to mellow as the gods and demons relaxed from their fighting to loll on the meadows of heaven. Then the male would come to the female's bedroom and court her before hours of frequent love play. The younger, attractive females were usually slender and sensuous in their movements. They walked with a swaying step, each finger sending a signal, each cock of the hip or stride of the thigh an invitation to the Shurian male. Since they did not give milk, the Shurian females had no breasts--that was one of the functions of the baba--but they had vestigial nipples, like the males, that helped arouse. The baba stayed out of sight during the Lissom Season, busy with last season's offspring.

Shurians mated much like humans, though the kjoni thing was higher up rather than part of the pissing area, and the male's organ was correspondingly half way to the navel, so that the motions and amount of effort were comparable to those of humans--as were the passions, the sounds, the promises, the endearments. Jory and Ramy secretly whispered about these matters as their changes began, but neither thought of the other in such a light.

At 13, Ramy was married in a great ceremony to a warrior prince, aged 15, of the Dumonhi family a day's journey along the Obayyo. They were a wealthy, powerful family, and the marriage was considered auspicious by both sides. The new husband ignored Jory all of the time, and Ramy most of the time, for he was a favorite son, and his father was training him to be a great general.

Everything about the babas was disgusting to Jory, no matter how they tried to placate him with gifts of human candy and shining fungal balls called honeyed sea foam that tasted subtly like caramel.

At least once each rotation of Shur around the gas giant, Ramy went to the quarters of her baba sister. There-- Jory had never been to those quarters, and didn't want to go--the two females did something where they lay down together--with much the same passions and sounds, and endearments and so forth--and the baba thrust a long, thin quill from her mouth deep into Ramy's neck. As Ramy lay paralyzed and enraptured, the baba slowly sucked out the fruits of Ramy's lovemaking with Dumonhi.

The baba would eat liberally at table--she was the favored recipient of the castle kitchen's stocks--and her babies would grow. After gestation, she would lie down while other babas tended to her. The newborns would slip out, encased in a transparent protein membrane. In more primitive times, the mother baba licked the membrane off and swallowed it--anything to feed her offspring. Nowadays, the attending babas would place the membrane on a ceramic plate and place it in a wall shrine with votive candles to Baba-Oba, the goddess of the world and of birth and of women. Ba meant 'sister,' and even the great island of life on Shur was named Oba.

If the birth was male, it might be one or two twin boys. If, on the other hand, the offspring were female, it was always one girl and one baba, not twins exactly, but very closely interwoven females, the baba being about twice the size of the egg-carrying baby. Thus, Ramy and her baba had been born. Every Shurian woman had her baba. In olden times, if the baba died, the sister was put to death. Nowadays it meant she would simply never marry, and she would have no status, but her life was respected nonetheless--and at least *nah* filth like humans were beneath her status. The system caused sisters to take excellent care of each other. This was why Jory and Ramy never thought that, even if she discovered their actions, Ramy's baba would betray them.

The men of Shurian society respected their babas as mothers, nurturers, witches, cooks, and so forth, but as adults hardly ever went near them. Men never slept with babas--that was the domain of their sisters. Shurians were amazed that humans could give birth to mixed male and female litters--further proof of their low animal natures. Shurians were also disgusted that human sex organs mingled physiologically with excretory organs. All three Shurian genders used the anus, situated like the human anus, for all excretion. The long ago sage had summed it up when he said: "To qif a lizard is to tenderize good meat for tomorrow's dinner. To qif a human is to qif what a lizard qifs."

Going to Kusi-O was the only way for him to stay alive, Jory could see. No matter how many ways he factored the equation, the outcome was always the same. Die here for sure, or risk dying there, but take a chance of living. Maybe escaping to the stars? Could one hope?

"Master, let's stop here for food and drink." Yafi leaned on his stick and pointed to a row of multicolored balls that glowed with fungal light--paper lanterns above a road shop.

"In my haste, I forgot to bring money," Jory said. The truth was, he was famished, and he must either die of hunger by the road side, or steal a cloak and start begging.

"My master has provided," Yafi said with a wink. "What is your taste? No expensive castle fare here."

"Any of the usual foods will do. You know what not to buy." Humans and Shurians could eat certain foods--the white tubers that were staple; the rice that grew in moon pools; many vegetables and pale night fruits; the meat of most quadrupeds on the island, which included dogs, cats, monkeys, and horses (so called by humans based on mythological animals of the supposed ancient Earth that had most likely never existed and was a fiction of groups like the Twelve Moon Society). Humans could die or get sick from certain things the Shurians ate with gusto-- small legged fishes with saw beaks that hid under rocks, spiders that pulsated and hummed to draw their victims in; bat-birds that flew at night and sucked blood; these were just some of the most deadly poisonous animals that Shurians ate raw. There were many dangerous fungi dishes also.

"Sit down and rest, Master. I will be back in a moment."

As the stranger walked with billowing robes toward the stand, Jory gauged the situation carefully. If Yafi planned to turn him in for a reward, he could already have done so. If he did not trust this brigand from the sewers of Anamo, what other way was there? Yafi disappeared like a phantom into the swirling mist. Jory watched his dark figure before the glowing stand as Shurians contemptuously slammed his purchases on the counter and took his coins as if they were dirty. Minutes later, Yafi returned holding a stiffened, folded paper tray with fragrant noodles and cooked white worms and some shreds of steamed meat in papered-rice wrappers. He also carried paper shells of soup, and from his wrist by a holder hung a disposable water jug.

"Thank you," Jory said sincerely.

"I thank you," Yafi said. "We must get you fixed up so that you will be safe and well. Here, Master, drink."

Jory drank deeply, noting a pleasant spicy taste, for the roadside inns often added a complementary taste to cover the staleness of water that had sat for a while. As warmth and satisfaction filled him, Jory felt the lightheadedness going away. For the first time in hours, he wasn't panting breathlessly. He noticed that Yafi kept looking furtively over his shoulders. Had there been time, he would have asked him why. But Jory's thoughts were on Ramy, with grave concern. She boiled in his stomach, as a Shurian might say.

Fog drifted by. Figures passed silently, leaning on sticks. The scene reminded Jory of a 1000kjir-old one-liner he'd learned at the court:

Evening fog, roadside
shop - colored lanterns
hang in no breeze.

Yafi rose.

"What is it?" Jory asked, noticing his own voice sounded funny--distant.

Yafi ignored him, stepping away as if expecting someone.

Jory knocked his tray of his lap in an effort to rise quickly, but he was paralyzed. He could not even speak in his anger and betrayal. He sat as if glued on the rock, and watched as several shadowy figures stepped out of the darkness.

Through blurry eyes, he saw the cloaked and hooded Yafi extend his hand. He saw a hand come out of another's cloak and place a bundle of imperial road money in Yafi's hand--the rustling paper notes tied with a string were unmistakable. Jory could not distinguish who the several big, cloaked figures were but he did notice two things--they all carried swords hidden by their cloaks, and the sleeve of the arm that had paid off Yafi was dark velvety brown, with silver Obayyo police officer's cuff-buttons indicating the Imperial service.

If Lord Ramyon's agents suspected a conspiracy, Jory thought as the light in his head faded, they had been right. But they had been wrong about the nature of the conspiracy--it wasn't about Jory escaping to Kusi-O or meeting with the Twelve Moon Society. If this involved the road police, it surely involved the Imperial palace.

No matter anymore to me, Jory thought dimly as he slipped helplessly sideways, landing on the damp gravel that smelled of horse droppings and rotting vegetables. No matter anymore to me or Ramy, he thought as her pale face shimmered in his memory, never again to be approached. The last things he was aware of were the bottoms of Yafi's feet as the latter ran away, having done his work, and a stick being roughly pushed into Jory's ribs. The Imperial police would treat him no better than would Lord Ramyon's soldiers, had they caught him first. He slipped into darkness, welcoming death if it should choose this moment to take him.

Lord Ramyon felt sick. He paced up and down at the window, ignoring the lovely distant vista. Only a distant foggy glow was visible of the Obayyo. Ramyon felt devastated-beyond anger, beyond betrayal.

First, he despaired of his poor judgment in keeping this overgrown lap monkey of a human. He should have castrated him and tossed him from the highest wall at the first sign of buckdom.

Worse, he wondered how he could bring himself to tell his son in law of the defilement. Or would word of ridicule sweep through all of Oba, bringing Lord Dumonhi the Elder down upon Castle Ramyon with his retainers and horde of barefoot warriors?

Ramyon was a proud man, and he would suffer the stings and snickers that would henceforth surround him even in his own castle. But the flower of his garden was now defiled, Ramy, his youngest. Had he erred with her somehow in her upbringing? Of course, by bringing the monkey to his court. That was the price of fad and fashion, he thought bitterly, he being a hard, leathery warrior who had often slept in the saddle and fought in the same saddle, having barely gotten off to squat. These women and their courtiers, he raged, pulling his sword. *Hal'ya!* he cried, whacking off the upper half of a woven basket. The steel sliced through as if the basket were made of air. Ramyon made a figure-eight twirling motion that snapped over his head like a pair of firecrackers, making the air hum briefly; in the same motion, he returned the sword to its scabbard.

Fingers tapped at the bottom of the rice paper screen separating his antechamber from the corridor. He could see the long claw-fingernails, low down, of a senior eunuch groveling on all fours.

"What is it?" He snapped. He'd meant to bellow, but his voice grew small at the thought that his flower was on her way, along with her baba. If there was any joy left in his soul, it now shriveled in the acids of his stomachs.

"Lord, the sisters."

It was a trusted male servant, and Ramyon remembered the leader's duty to cultivate loyalty through the four virtues--kindness, rightness, honesty, and unbendingness. "Wait one minute, then bring them in and leave us alone." Ramyon went to his raised dais and sat cross-legged on the huge pillow there.

"Thank you, Master," breathed the servant in relief, probably glad not to have his eardrums flayed, nor to witness what might happen in this room.

The door slid soundlessly open, and two tearful figures hobbled in, prostrating themselves before the dais. Ramy-ba and Ramy-baba wailed and raised their arms beseechingly. Their faces were contorted with weeping and moaning.

Ramyon fumbled with the wooden gavel at his side and swung blindly, just catching the Call to Order gong. Several servants in the corridor scrambled like rats being flushed out. "Privacy!" Ramyon bellowed. Then to the two females: "Silence!"

Ramy stayed on her knees, face pressed to the carpeted wooden floor in her hands so that her fingers dripped with tears and snot. She sobbed continuously and convulsively, trembling in fear all the while. The baba sat upright like a monolith, holding her hands over her face in shame and mortification, for it was she who had reported the trysts to the Mistress baba, sister of Ramyon's wife. They had taken charge, the babas, as unfortunately was their right, before he could intervene, and the result was this bleak chaos.

The ancient sage had lamented:

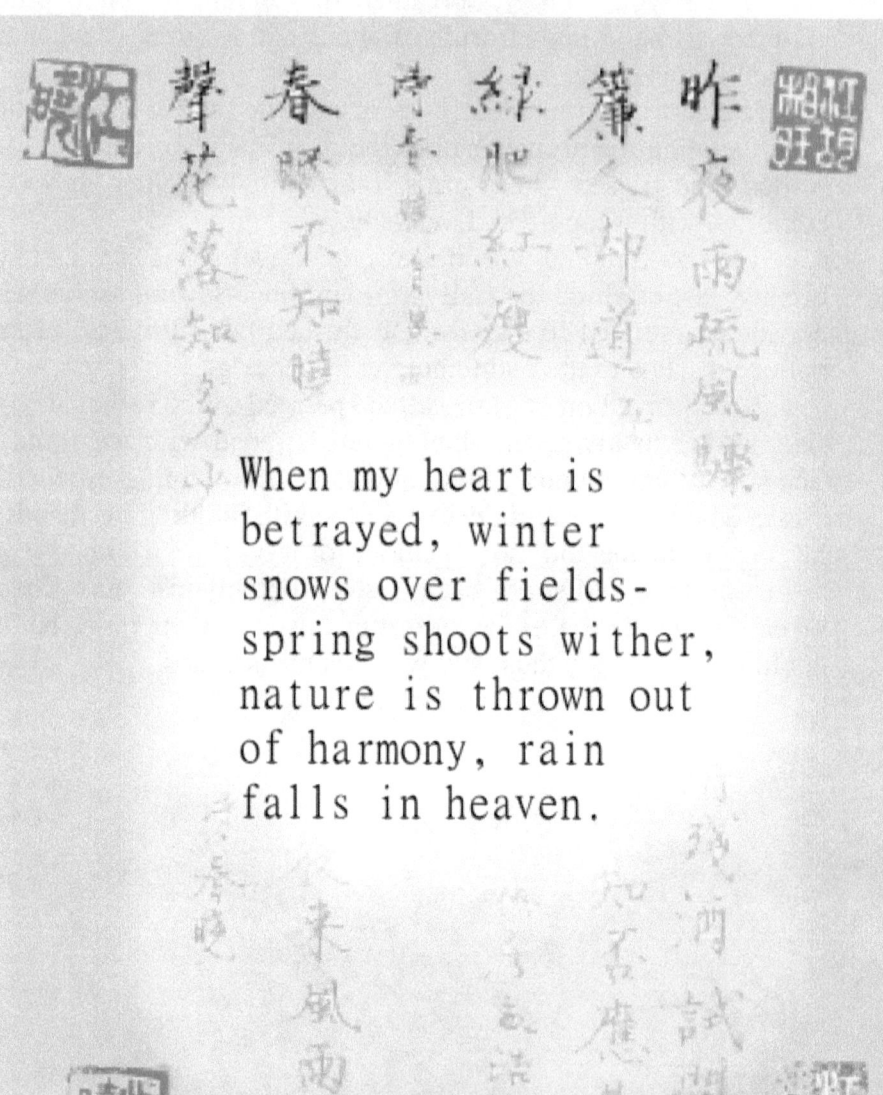

When my heart is
betrayed, winter
snows over fields-
spring shoots wither,
nature is thrown out
of harmony, rain
falls in heaven.

As he stared at his daughters, Ramyon became speechless. He boiled with suffering and anger, until he bit down on his protruding tongue. It was a Shurian's way of expressing anguish upon betrayal by a loved one. He would bite his tongue until the pain equaled that in his heart. Then he would say what he had to say before the tongue swelled his mouth shut, so that he long could not speak.

"You fools," Ramy heard Father speak chokingly. After a long taut silence in the gloomy room, he spoke of the sisters' late mother. "The only blessing tonight is that your mother and her saintly baba are in paradise and do not know these things you have done within this air they gave you to breathe."

Ramy looked up startled at the sudden sound of his voice, as if someone had poked her with a sharp object.

"You," Father said to the baba, "what jealousy possessed you? Did you want the monkey's mouth on yours also?"

"No, Father!" the baba wailed in her syrup-thick, almost masculine voice.

Ramy sighed as Father yelled at her sister.

All three of them knew that she loved her baba, and that the baba was as much her spouse as was young Lord Dumonhi.

Ramy blamed herself as the First Cause. She had seduced her loyal, gentle companion, Jory, out of some inner anger at Dumonhi, not so much because he was mostly away, but because when he made love he was callous as if he were milking cattle.

Now she had brought the wrath of the Universe down. She understood the outcome.

Best case, and least likely, she would have her tongue cut off and be sent into exile at a far monastery, to live silently in a cell alone.

Worst case, her father would kill both her and the baba any moment now.

In any case, poor Jory would die. Judging by the way his scabbarded sword lay loosely by Father's side, and by the condition of the large linen-storage basket, their lives had no value anymore.

"And you, Cause of Celestial Disharmony!"

She felt the hurt inside his anger, and knelt upright, buttocks resting on her heels.

She wiped her face with the ends of her plain linen robe and said: "Whatever my fate, I accept it, Father. I only have the wish to tell you once more that I love you and I am sorry I caused this hurt."

As she spoke, she stared at his fearsome face, his huge eyes and rippling jaws like a dragon's--and only understood his silence when thick blood flowed from the downturned corners of his mouth. His eyes were wild holes, and blood spiderwebbed on his clothing.

The baba threw her hands up and wailed anew.

Ramy jumped up and ran to wipe his mouth with the hem of her long robe.

But he rose.

The sword flashed in the air. He froze in a gesture as if to slice her in half down the middle, which he easily could have, as he had once slain his enemies in battle--and some of them in leather or wooden armor!

She knelt on the floor directly before the dais, opened her robe at the chest, and pulled it back to expose her neck.

She inclined her head deeply, until her forehead touched the floor, and waited for the sound of the wind.

Instead, he threw himself back on his pillow, groaning with pain, and tossed the sword aside. "What have you done to me, you garden weed?"

"I have brought disgrace to our family and to my future husband's."

"Ah well do you know it, viper." He pulled the decapitated basket close and took out a linen towel to staunch his blood. He spoke in a halting, painfully slurry voice: "I should throw you both out that window. But you, foolish wasp"--he used the human word to wound the baba--"you useless spider, because you could not be discreet in your insect-like spitefulness, this matter will be the laughing stock of the Obayyo for the next thousand kjirs.

"Worse by far, Dumonhi will not fall for it for a moment.

"Ah dammit, a pox on you both. If he were here, he could honorably wound his shame by killing you with his bare hands or any way he chooses, as is his right. I should probably pen you up like animals until he returns from the campaign on Far Tomi Shore. Your fate will be most unpleasant, for he may turn you both over to their family babas, and I cannot imagine what they will invent by way of torturing you both to death."

A moment of horrified silence filled the room, as each contemplated a picture of several large, wasp-like females with many legs and arms, busily stabbing, piercing, burning, and biting Ramy and Ramy-baba toward a long, agonizing death.

It need not come to that, of course, for there were the knives of love, the knives of the rabbit.

Ramy sensed her father's continued love, even amid his torment and loss. She spoke with dignity, as befitted a Ramyon noblewoman. She addressed her father in a high, even voice, for everything was suddenly very clear.

Even the pain, the loneliness, the abandonment that Dumonhi's callousness had caused her had evaporated.

She felt sorry for Jory, and wished him life, perhaps as a bandit if he escaped. Dumonhi notwithstanding, Jory was the only male she had ever loved as a lover, though her father thought of him as a monkey.

"Father, we will commit astound the rabbit by dawn this very night." She meant that she and her baba would commit suicide together with their nursery knives, given so long ago.

The silence in the room was as profound as the black shadows that flooded the corners and the floor around her knees. Her sister was a dark mound in the darkness.

Father rose, wiping his mouth with the spattered linen. Leaving his sword thrown aside, he stepped shakily from the dais and bent close to look at Ramy for the last time. His expression was a mixture of fury and pain. A trail of tears ran down the creases in each cheek. He held the towel before his mouth and could no longer speak. But he touched her cheek lightly with the backs of two fingers.

She touched herself there and found blood on her fingertips.

She licked her fingers and tasted his forgiveness, which filled her like a spring breeze.

He touched her baba similarly, forgiving her also.

The sister, or wasp, bowed before her maker. She was a large, coppery shape half-draped in amber shadows, with a Shurian face and upper body, but a carapace and half-insect legs in back.

Had Ramy married Dumonhi, they would have begotten together. He would have fertilized Ramy, who would have fertilized the eggs carried in her sister. The baba would have birthed--in the Tower of Babas, assisted by the other holy babas--one baby and one tiny new matching baba in each delivery. That was how life had evolved on Oba, and now Ramy had tampered with the laws of the cosmos and the gods.

Lord Ramyon--without ever looking on his daughters again-- turned his back and stormed out of the room to his private chambers.

Servants slid the doors shut, leaving the two sisters in moonlit isolation.

Silence. The audience chamber was an antechamber of death. Moonlight brooded in lacquer surfaces. The room smelled of wax and flowers.

Ramy-baba's mind was awhirl with horror. She had betrayed her lover and sister, and condemned herself and Ramy to death. She had brought mockery and war upon Ramyon. Had it been worth this to hurt her sibling over a romantic jealousy? Ramy-baba was deeply ashamed, and sat waiting for her sister's sharp words.

Both sighed.

"Forgive me, sister," Ramy-baba at last said.

"What have you done?"

"I wish I could undo it, but now I can't."

After a long silence, Ramy said: "We must prepare for death." She rose. "I have to go to my room and tidy things up."

Ramy-baba shifted her bulk erect. "Will I see you again?"

"I will come to your chamber when I have composed myself."

"I pray that you do."

She watched as Ramy walked with small steps.

Ramy-baba said brokenly: "I do not have the courage to die alone, my love."

Ramy's steps slowed briefly. She did not look back. "You should have thought of this before your evil tongue wagged, sister."

"I will go last," Ramy-baba said. "It is the least I can do."

"It is as if we had never lived," Ramy said as she reached the door.

"You loved," Ramy-baba said. "Therefore, you have lived. I can only say that I loved you, my sister."

Ramy stood gripping the doorway, prepared to collapse if her sister said the cruel words: *But you loved a monkey.*

Before the baba could speak, Ramy said: "He is of a different species, but much like we are, or greater. They once ruled the galaxy. Now they are our floor mats and night buckets. But he is more a man than Dumonhi will ever be."

"We have nothing to fear," Ramy-baba said, "so we may speak freely. Whomever you love, I love. I love your man with you, even though he and I may never touch or speak."

Ramy nodded curtly. She wanted to thank her baba, but words could not cross her lips. So wrenched was her soul.

Ramy slid the door open, let herself out, and slid the door almost closed, leaving Ramy-baba the option to leave the room if she chose. What did anything really matter now?

She gathered her strength and rushed through the dark hallway toward her rooms, to prepare for the end.

Ramy-baba suffered similar thoughts and sentiments.

What would anything matter in a few hours when they were in the Celestial Hall?

Ramy-baba felt so weak, she might just sit here the rest of her time.

Then, ashamed in the face of her sister's courage and determination, she walked down dark corridors, over the creaking wooden bridge-floor, and into the babas' tower.

There, the doors were closed as the other babas slept.

She went to her room, which was large and had a window view, since she was an important baba despite her youth.

Sobbing, she straightened her possessions--her amulets; small clay figurines including some cute ones and some frightening ones for warding off evil spirits; jewelry, perfumes, fungi preparations for her skin and her egg-pipette.

When there was nothing left to do, she lay down on the bed and pondered the incredible reversal of her fate. She thought about the other babas.

There were terrible jealousies among the wasps. Many hated Ramy-baba because she domineered them as was her right by caste order.

They would deal with her harshly if she lived into the coming days; better to go now, quietly, to have been without saying goodbye, just to have been and then not to be.

Long before the first milky green fingers of dawn rose over the horizon, there was a rustle of silk.

Ramy-baba turned in joyful anticipation as Ramy hurried into the room.

Ramy wore her best gown meant for the wedding ceremonies, and Ramy-baba assumed Ramy would want her husband to see her for the last time like this before they buried her.

Ramy-baba turned away and hung her head. "Will you forgive me?"

She felt Ramy's arms steal around her from behind.

"Who else can I turn to, foolish baba?"

Ramy-baba turned and gave back an embrace, so that they were entwined, the one sister much larger than the other. "We have so little time.

"By dawn, the others will be awake. We will be at their mercy," Ramy said.

"We will be quick and merciful," Ramy-baba said. With longing, she ran her pudgy fingers and droopy arms up and down Ramy's slender back.

Ramy waited passively, her hands on her sister's shoulders, her breathing coming quicker.

Ramy-baba groaned with desire as her palms burned on the smooth waist and oval buttocks, the sharp hip bones and long shapely thighs of her sister.

"Go make the bed," Ramy-baba whispered, sending her sister off with a lingering palm on one buttock.

She watched as Ramy walked away loosening her wedding dress with two hands on a button behind her back. She left the ceremonial belt knotted, however. Watching her, the baba salivated and her heart pounded.

As the baba fixed their bed, Ramy cleared a pewter jug and some cups from the fruit table by the window.

Ramy opened the bay windows and arched back her back with two pressuring hands while staring into the predawn of Shur.

A red moon hung like a distant lantern over the sea.

Fog swirled like milk far below on the Obayyo, the Lantern Road.

Already, birds twittered and thrashed in the highest tree crowns. Dew dripped like a steady heartbeat on a tin barrel cover out on the stone balconies.

Ramy-baba pulled a mattress from the bench box under the windows, and unrolled it on the table.

Meanwhile, Ramy prettied herself at the mirror near the window. She fluffed her cloud of orange hair, and smoothed fragrances over her glassy skin. How much she looked like a monkey human, Ramy-baba thought enviously. She wondered if there were some interspecies strain, some dark and hidden helix, entwined with Ramy's Shurian genes.

Who knew what bred under the stars, across so much time and distance? The babas were experts on breeding--it was their function in Oba's hot-house climate, where the dominant species were trisexual.

Ramy-baba quietly went to the other end of the long room.

Careful lest Ramy see, the baba took a velvet bundle from a secret drawer

She unrolled the bundle, exposing two special knives. Each knife had a long handle of intricately carved ivory, suitable for a woman to hold with both hands and sweep slowly sideways pushing with all the strength of one forearm.

Each blade was extremely pointed for a quick puncture, and very sharp, but wide to pressure the organs and keep them apart.

Engraved on each hilt was a poem from the Ancient Bard, in archaic language, carved in elegant Oba High Period calligraphy--a poem fit for the occasion of a double departure from life.

I must be brave for both of us now, thought the baba to herself as she prepared their bed of love and death.

She hid the two swords of duello where she would find them at the right moment.

That moment would come when Ramy, in her orgasm, would forget life itself while thrashing wildly amid cries of passion.

Despite herself, the baba knew she must sacrifice her own final throes. It was a punishment almost too terrible to bear, but she owed this to her sister.

After that, the rest would be quick, and the eternal rest blissful.

When she was done, she held the two swords in her hands. Before summoning her sister, she contemplated the order of the universe, prayed to her personal gods and baba-deities, and marveled at how the cosmos always restored order to itself, no matter what. That was the wisdom of Rabbit-in-the-Grass, innocent but powerful messenger of the gods. Children came to know him and love him, and he in turn was their guardian messenger throughout life.

Invoking an innocent nursery tale, fit for the beginning of life rather than its end, one sword said the first thing, while the other sword said the last thing, fit for life's ending.

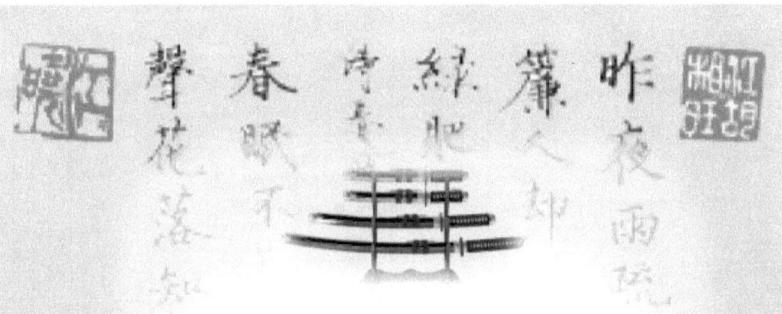

Two moons embrace
above the koh tree.

Celestial dome turns,
hiding moons behind
tree trunk.

Rabbit-in-the-Grass
catches his breath -
will reappear soon?

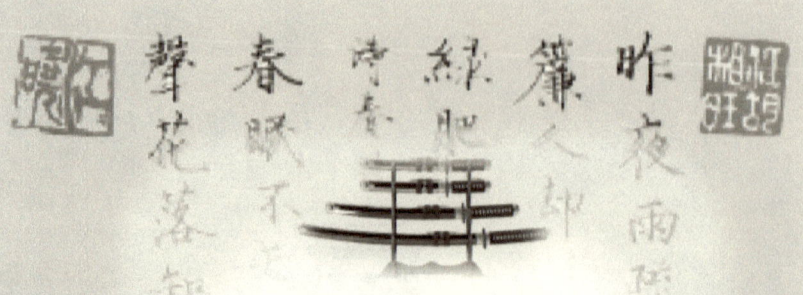

Celestial dome turns,
revealing what hid
behind the koh.

Not a single moon
in sight,
alas.

Rabbit-in-the-Grass
sighs and hops away.

Loosely bundling the knives in their blue velvet cloth, Ramy-baba trundled over to the table.

Ramy had dropped her clothes on the floor and lay naked in the dim light. The slender curves of her youthful body, and her long legs, glowed with a faint milky-blue light. She lay on her left side facing away, the curving shadow between her buttocks a mysterious valley. Her right leg was pulled up slightly, laying a curved knee upon a knee that was nearly straight. Everything was exactly as tradition dictated it must be on earth and in heaven.

Ramy-baba stared long. She was not a poetess, but she wanted to capture this last divine vision in every detail. She wanted to remember it like a perfect poem well told as the knife made its journey from east to west.

Ramy's arms extended over her head, elbows in her orange hair that was fluffed out to accept the full scent and breeze of the night. On each side of her chest was a dark wrinkled spot, a nipple useless as that of a man, but exquisitely tender to the touch of both lovers.

Ramy-baba took great care to lay her bundle down without making a sound. Then she advanced upon her sister like a shadow. She noticed that Ramy lay with her face toward the moonlight, and her blue tongue was slightly extended in pleasure.

Ramy-baba touched a nipple with her own blue tongue, and Ramy's tongue slid further out. The two sisters lay together, the larger spooning the smaller, who writhed while the other alternately ran her palms and fingertips over and over the same hills and valleys until Ramy turned, and from there it was a language of tongues, of roving fingers, until finally, when the foam-sea could no longer be denied, Ramybaba mounted one brown leg over her sister's waist and held Ramy's head in her fingertips. The pipette extended from baba's upper palate. It was long as a finger when fully extended, and stained in various shades of brown and gray. It was hollow, and sheathed in a thin layer of skin and nerve endings that made a glow of passion and desire in Ramy-baba's head as she closed her eyes and sought the tiny bony protrusions on either side of Ramy's neck. Ramy groaned with anticipation, flailing her wrists passionately against her sister's massive shoulders as the beak found its way into the protrusion, parting a sphincter there, and sinking down into the spongy tissue that contained love's fluids. As the shaft entered, it released a fungal poison that acted as a powerful stimulant. Ramy uttered a series of high, choking moans while struggling to breathe at the same time. Her body, held tenderly by her sister, convulsed in erotic spasms. Ramy-baba, too, was utterly aroused. The same fungal release made her blind with desire as she tensed her normally flaccid body for the receipt of fertilized eggs. The eggs would fall together into the womb near baba's center, where over nine months the next son or pair of sisters would form.

While she was still high from their shared orgasm--in fact, while the beak was still in Ramy's pleasure hole, and Ramy was half-conscious--the baba whispered "I love you" and began strangling her sister. "This is the best way, my beloved," she whispered as she made her fingers ever tighter, until at last she felt Ramy go limp. Then she reached for the knife to finish the first of two duellos, slicing the belly as swiftly as a sunset.

Ramy-baba dismounted and threw her robe loosely over her body. She did not want to be found naked--men and non-sisters would be revulsed at her appearance. If the woman-sister was beautiful as a star in her man's eyes, the baba was ungainly like the earth.

The Ancient Sage had written:

Baba is unpleasant soil
yet she mothers flowers
honored in heaven.

Still weak and in shock, Ramy-baba staggered around the table for a last look at her dead sister. Ramy's hands lay limp together. Her legs would never run again. Her eyes stared sightlessly into the sky, whose first tendril of light made her eyes glitter. Her face had a vacant, slightly shocked expression. Her tongue had turned from blue to black and hung fully extended from her red lips like a dark worm on the marble tabletop, where the mattress had slid aside during their love making.

Ramy-baba arranged the body, which was still warm, but cooling rapidly. First she used a long linen bandage to hold the burst organs in. She worked the body into the wedding dress and laid it on its back. She folded Ramy's hands on her chest and straightened Ramy's legs, and put tiny white slippers on the bare feet. She wept softly all the while.

Then she sat down and composed herself. She tried to listen to the sound of her heart, but there was too much rushing in her ears. She chose the knife with the two moons because it spelled hope. Still composing herself, she held the knife before her and stared at it in an effort to make it enter her torso more easily. She stared at it long and thoughtfully, weighing her sins and praying to the gods and goddesses who waited for her, most of all Ramy who had just become an ancestor-god.

The castle was silent as the bottom of a pond.

They would give her as long as she needed, presumably on order of Lord Ramyon. She was a non-person, half dead already. She sat for a time, testing the knife's heft, balancing it in one hand, then the other. Slowly, she brought the point to her belly.

The fungal poison had sickened Jory O'Call to the verge of death, not a whit closer. He recognized the dark touch of the babas as he lay vomiting watery soup laced with twirling bits of vegetal matter into a bucket. For a while, he was too sick to care where he was, or even that the place smelled bad like rancid butter. Fire inside and outside tormented him as he threw up what mean gruel or rabbit food was brought to him.

After what seemed like an eternity, probably a few days, a Fril woman came with a warm, wet towel. She knelt by his bedside and wiped his cheeks, showing him the white fungal deposits that covered the area around his mouth. "You will be feeling better now," she said in a curious snapping voice. She spoke Human fair enough, but strangely. Jory glimpsed the inside of her mouth as she spoke--toothless mustard-colored gums; a narrow, longish tongue split at the tip; and a round throat hole that he suspected she liked to distend of an evening now and then while she enjoyed a large river rat or two. Indeed, her skin was snake-like--dry, flaking here and there, colored in equal sized patches of white, dull silver, and light yellow. Her nostrils were a pair of slits, her eyes black buttons over which gray nictitating membranes slid horizontally from either corner. Her manner was kind, however, and Jory had lived with worse in the babas. Her hands--same colors, same scaly raspy skin, and an opposing thumb plus three flat-tipped fingers-- were gentle in their touch. "You must not give yourself away," she said in her thick accent, "nor us, or we will all die on Oba Island."

"Believe me, I don't want that. Am I safe here?"

"You are as safe as a human can be under these circumstances."

"But I am in Kusi-O?" His chest constricted at the thought he might not be.

"You are. This is Kusi-O. My husband and I keep an inn here. We have been paid well to keep you safe."

"Who pays you?" He must know. Why would anyone want a court poet so badly?

She chuckled. "You find out soon enough. Now you rest and get better."

"How did you get me in through the gates?" The thick concrete drum surrounding Kusi-O was actually a five story building with walls so smooth even a lizard could not climb them. The building had no windows at all. It had several gates that, most of the time, acted like airlocks--if the Oba side was open, the Kusi-O side was shut, and vice versa. Goods coming from either side were left in the open corridor between the two worlds. Both gates were again shut. Then the receiving gate opened and a flock of cargo slaves rushed in, supervised by armed warriors-- Imperial road police on the Oba side, Fril cops on the Kusi-O side. The system had worked for centuries, bringing wealth in and Shurian goods out, while keeping the status at quo and the wealthy in power.

"That is a secret," the snake woman said. "Rest. It will be days before you are able to walk without getting dizzy. Oba grannies' poison is very potent but works well." She emitted what passed for a giggle and fled toward the wooden door. The Fril wore little in the way of clothing. She wore only a loincloth and had small breasts. He wondered if she carried her eggs inside until they hatched. Frankly, he did not care. As long as he was still alive... then he thought of Ramy, and burst into tears.

The innkeeper was Girex, his wife Giru. They were quiet, kind people whose only child was severely disabled in a special clinic on their home planet. They welcomed a little gaxba, 'so-so money,' on the side to send home. Each time they did, it meant their child could receive special medicine and be released home a time with a nurse. Jory did not ask--he did not want to pry. What if they sold him back to the Oba road police for a higher price after they finished receiving payments from the unknown parties in Kusi-O? He kept an eye out for treachery, but they must be good actors indeed if they meant to betray him. No, as long as he was in their inn, he could say they harbored him, and they would be delivered to the Obayyo officials in wooden stocks, ready for the chopping block.

He stayed in what once had been a giant chimney. His bed and a few items of furniture were on a sandy floor. The odor of whatever had burned here, kjirs ago, still clung faintly to the walls like a decaying cheese. The walls appeared dry, except for traces of ubiquitous Oba fungi. Jory recognized a dozen kinds amid cracks in the white plaster, on blunt rock surfaces where plaster had fallen off, and in the interstices where heavy structural beams poked through. Where the thick, low wooden door now hung, which Girex and Giru had to bow to walk through, had once been a steel furnace door.

As the fire in his gut healed, Jory became aware of the source of what, in his sickness, he had thought of as fire surrounding him with pain: Light. The light at the bottom of the chimney had a bluish cast. When he peered upward in fascination, the chimney's top disappeared into what looked like a vortex of blue-white light.

"We on Fril enjoy direct sunlight," Girex told Jory one afternoon. Girex was bigger than his wife, and more powerfully built, but just as gentle. Both seemed to have a faint deviousness about them that made Jory wonder if it was an invention of his mind, or a property of persons who looked like snakes. But it was open, not hidden, and maybe it was just their sense of shame and guilt about deceiving the authorities and risking death for a sum of money.

Girex helped Jory climb up within the old chimney. A wide, sturdy ladder stretched some forty feet upward. Jory climbed ahead, while Girex followed, coaxing him on. "Hold on tight," he admonished.

"Ah!" Jory gasped with pain and averted his face. The blue-white light burned his eyes like a searing sun.

"You'll have to go slowly," Girex said, "Your eyes were made to enjoy the beautiful light."

Yes, Jory thought bitterly, not to be enslaved by people who live in perpetual night. There was an expression on Oba: 'Blind as a crx,' a kind of fungus-eating mole. Shurians were just as likely to say "blind as a human."

"You will become accustomed to the beautiful light," Girex said as they climbed back down. "There are spy holes up there where you can look without being seen. They will be your only glimpse of this place before you leave for deep space."

"Deep space," Jory said slowly. "I have heard that ships travel from star to star."

Girex waved his arm contemptuously. "It is a dark age on the other side of the wall. Ships do not travel to stars--they would burn up. They travel to moons, like Shur, or planets, like Fril. You will learn all these things soon enough."

"So who has paid you for me, and what do they want from me?"

Girex raised his hands, empty. "I don't know. I don't care. I think you are different from the other humans. They say you have horns." He gingerly reached for one of Jory's temples. "Are they broken off?"

"I have never had horns," Jory said. "This is something else." The other humans had laughed at him and shied away from him because of them. Now even this snake was acting as if there were something wrong with him. He brushed Girex's hand away.

"It must be something expensive else," Girex said with lewd nerviness.

Jory would soon learn the source of Girex's strange behavior. In the meantime, he ate well. He exercised as best he could to build up his strength-- the heavy poison had left him strangely weak for a young man, but he felt his energy rebounding. Every few hours, he practiced climbing up the ladder and tried to accustom himself to the brightness outside.

Girex watched him and laughed. "That's not even real daylight. Wait until you step onto a real planet with two or three suns in a white sky."

The intense light in Kusi-O was caused by an imported power unit that sat in the center of the mile-diameter circle wall. Girex explained that the hydrogen powered helium chewer, as he called it, glowed through a thick, milky wall of glass two palms thick. Still there was enough energy left to pipe light through glass cables, out to the wall on all sides, up the wall, where it shone down from hundreds of spotlights. The substitute sunlight was evenly distributed and could burn for ages.

Jory spent many hours staring from the narrow slits on all sides of the old chimney, which had provided energy centuries ago before Kusi-O had received the benefit of nuclear lighting. He had to keep from sneezing half the time, and often brushed cobwebs from his head. He had to keep an eye out for the silently crawling red and black striped spiders whose sting was venomous; the others were merely annoying. From his vantage point, Jory saw in all directions.

He saw the looming drum wall, its surfaces soiled with long stains of dampness and moss. Several times a day, the great gate closest to him would open on the Obayyo. Sometimes, in the gloom of the inner wall, he could see the gleam of the Imperial police armor and swords while near-naked Fril cops with spidery looking black vap guns stood on this side. Pallet upon pallet of urns and trunks of various sizes arrived from points all over Oba, to be shipped to the worlds serviced by the Raum Transport League.

Toward the center of Kusi-O, Jory made out the dimly glowing milky-glass dome of the light generator. Around that on all sides were the landing pads for antigrav shuttles. The gray, boxy shuttles looked beat-up, and were streaked with chemical and burn marks. Their experienced, bored pilots snapped them through fast take-offs and landings.

Around the ring of pads was a ring of warehouses. Through the warehouses moved tons of material, mostly the thousands of varieties of fungal extracts, but also some fine swords and other cultural oddities.

In a ring around the inside of the Wall, and inside a wide circumferential dirt road, were the houses of Kusi-O's permanent residents. There must be as many as 5,000, Jory thought, and they not only lived in homes but sent their children to schools, and went to parks, and frequented libraries and public-houses like the one where Jory hid.

As Jory's eyes became used to the light, he was amazed that he'd ever tolerated the gloom that seemed to pour in when the gate was open. Once he saw a captured human--a wild man with long hair, dirty skin, and tattered clothes--dragged to the gate in chains by Fril police and handed over to the Imperial police, who immediately placed wooden blocks around the unfortunate's neck. Jory might be next.

Jory saw all sorts of beings from the far reaches of space. He saw things stranger than the Fril--floating orbs that bore sentient life; tall yellow things with dangling appendages, that he'd swear could only live in the sea; four legged and even eight-limbed mammals covered with fur or feathers; a slug-like thing that took all day to move its glistening brown sausage shape along the road from one warehouse to another.

Girex and Giru's behavior became stranger and stranger, and Jory became alarmed. At times the house remained shuttered, with drunken customers pounding on the front door in the middle of the night demanding food and liquor. At other times, the pub seemed to be open long past the customary hour, and carousing customers kept Jory awake all night.

Jory, locked in his chimney around the clock, became jumpy. He'd cling to the door for hours at a time, listening for a certain type of footfall. Even when it was only Giru with his meals, he ran up the ladder like a frantic animal, though he had no hope of fighting a group of Fril police if they came for him.

Then, one night, Jory's fears seemed to come true. He heard heavy leather boots tread in the corridor. He heard the murmur of men's voices, none too pleasant, and the clink of metal objects--keys? He jumped up from his cot and, in the faint moonlight-like glow of the generator outside, ran to the ladder and up several steps, thinking maybe he could jump down on them.

The door opened, and several men stepped inside. "There he is," said a Fril holding a black gun, pointing with his free hand. There were five, two of them naked Fril, the other three wearing voluminous dark cloaks that just about reached the floor. These swept back baggy hoods to reveal Fril-like heads. All five wore the tokens of immunity--flat name tags suspended against the chest by a thin chain that ran around the neck--promising freedom from Imperial search or detention, as long as they stayed within the port and did not wander out somehow into dark Oba.

Jory was paralyzed with fear. He could almost feel the Obayyo cops' heavy wooden tablets around his neck, with the legend "Runaway--Sentence Is Death" carved on them.

"Are you Jory O'Call?" asked one of the three in cloaks.

Jory climbed up another rung and did not answer.

"We won't hurt you," said another. "You are the reason we are here."

"We?" Jory asked. "Where's Girex? Giru?"

"Look, friend, we don't have time..." The leader swept off his imitation Fril hood, revealing a human, a young adult with short brown hair and pale skin. The other two cloaked men pulled their disguises off. One was dark and had short, kinky black hair--Jory had seen a few like him around other villages, not his own. The third was of medium color, with slanted eyes and short black hair cut in such a fashion that it stood straight up. They looked strong and well-fed-- no slaves, these, ever, from their self-confident demeanor. "I'm Jerzy." Jerzy introduced the black one as Hans, and the hair-up as Don.

Jerzy said: "Come on down; we've got to get you out of here."

At the sight of his fellow humans, Jory bounded down and shook their hands. They whisked a cloak and a Fril mask over him, threw the hood over his head, and hurried him into the dark halls. Guns drawn and shielding him on three sides, they moved in a mass.

"Where are Girex and Giru?" Jory asked.

"Ah, those scum..." Don said.

"Look briefly," Jerzy said, pointing into a room
from which yellow light fell.

Hans said: "They were well-paid, all right. A little too well."

Jory looked inside, heart beating in horror, and saw his hosts. Girex was sprawled in one corner, white powder strewn over his head and brightening his hands. Giru lay on her back, sprawled and staring emptily at the ceiling. She too had streaks of powder all over. "Are they--?"

"Dead. Yes," Jerzy said. "They were drug addicts. That's how the local goons paid them to take care of you. Paid them with so much of that stuff that they overdosed until their hearts stopped. They must have been crawling on the floor throwing it in the air in their last moments."

Jory could think of at least twelve drugs it could be, all made in Oba by the babas, capable of addicting half a galaxy.

"Maybe someone wanted them out of the way," Don ventured.

"Naw," said one of the Fril, "too valuable. Must be suicide. Too much overdose. Kill. Stupid ones. Find other, but these trustworthy."

Jerzy pushed on. "We weren't planning to pull you out so soon, but the Dora Mora is in orbit, and several of her boats have set down. With these two gone, it's only a matter of hours before the cops start poking around. They are required to file a report with the other side. Come along, the ship's master is eager to pick you up."

The five figures spirited Jory away in a car that smelled of fish or snakes or something. One of the real Fril drove. It was trip of a few minutes. The noisy clatter of the space port grew louder and enveloped them as the car turned down short streets. When the car halted, there was a furtive payment, an exchange of sharp, thin light beams full of official seals, and the humans hustled Jory out by his elbows. The Fril took off with the car. Jory stood before a sea of lights in whose center rested the grav-assist boat that would take him to space.

Jory was amazed at the bustle of the cargo boat that was ten or more stories tall. He entered with his companions and stood on a dirty steel floor in a low-ceilinged corner crammed with bio-electronic devices and displays. Jory stared in fascination at all this wonderful machinery that had been locked out of Oba for centuries.

Jory saw that the cargo bay occupied most of the boat's interior. Broad bulkheads were open, and Fril and other alien laborers worked around the clock loading the boat for its trip into orbit to join the Dora Mora. The noise of generators, voices, and loaders was deafening. The interior bay was 200 arm spans long, 100 arm spans wide, and 40 arm spans high. The ceiling was slightly curved outward and reinforced on the inside with steel beams that had circles cut out for lightness. Bright biolume strips streaked the ceiling and the walls with a light so bright in some places that it was bluish.

In that moment, a small worm of determination settled in Jory's soul. If he were ever able, he would come back and smash those gates. He would tear down that concrete drum wall. He would free not only the humans on Oba, but the Shurians from themselves.

"This way," Jerzy said, grabbing a handful of Jory's cloak. He pulled, and Jory and the other two men followed. They bolted up a narrow, claustrophobic metal stairwell that rang with their footsteps. On the second floor, they entered a doorway that led to a series of narrow rooms or cabins set into the boat's walls, whose windows overlooked the loading bay. Jerzy locked the door behind them, while Don pulled the dark blue curtains on the windows closed. There was one virtual window to see space once they took off. The room was carpeted in dark red, and had a kitchen built into the other end from where Jory stood. A door at the other end led, he supposed, to more rooms like this one, places for the crew or maybe the officers to rest while the boat was under way.

"About ten hours," Jerzy said, "and she'll be lifting off."

They pulled off their disguises and threw them over a set of couches set in one corner. The three spacemen wore the ubiquitous uniform of the bipedals--a loose fitting cotton jumpsuit that opened down the front and had many small pockets to keep things when gravity was at a premium. Jerzy's was a faded khaki, Don's a new dark blue, Hans's a dim light blue. Hans and Don threw themselves back on the worn but comfortable looking brown couches along the outer wall. Jerzy headed for the corner sink. Jory stared at the soft lighting, and the smooth waves it made on the creamy, plastic-coated ceilings. He welcomed a host of clean, human smells. These men took everything for granted while, for him, every moment meant a new sensation.

He hardly noticed the door that opened or the woman who walked into the room.

She had to speak his name twice before he looked at her, startled.

She was pretty, that he could see. Her skin was dusky brown. Her hair was puffy like the Shurians', but black and thick, with many fine curls, and cropped just beyond the ears so it made a fluffy helmet. Her eyes were serious, light blue and playful. Her jumpsuit was new and clean, brown like a tree trunk. Jory liked the way her hips moved in the suit, and her unassuming breasts were high and firm. She moved with style and authority. "I'm happy to see you, Jory O'Call." She extended a small hand whose nails she'd painted glossy rouge. Her grip was light but firm. Official. "I'm Josenda Kellahi. I'll be your official guardian until you join the crew of Dora Mora."

Jory nodded, enjoying her warmth and light smile. He noted the light pink lipstick, the several tiny gold rings in her cheeks, the small pink bow attached to her high forehead. He also noted with surprise that she packed a huge black gun in a dark green holster on a wide web belt with small military-looking pouches. On the left chest surface of her overalls were insignia patches suggesting she could shoot, run, wrestle, and fight with the best of them.

"We'll be taking off in six bells," she said. "They are loading the heavy cargo bottom first. Ten tons of special Oba core-soil for a royal pleasure garden on Rorath IV." She grinned. "Where there's a need, we go. You'll probably enjoy the Service." Seeing his confused, numb look, she added: "Of course you're entitled to quit if you wish. Just--don't before Captain Aptath has had a chance to present you with a proposal." She had a crisp, athletically attractive, almost handsome face. The softness of her skin, the curvature of her cheeks, and the twinkle of her lipstick made her look pretty and feminine. He liked looking at her, in this wealth of wonderful light, as her features kept pulling between the athletically hard and feminine soft.

Jory sat on the couch while she stepped beside Jerzy at the sink to prepare steaming hot cups of something for them--*kjaba*, they called the bitter but savory black brew whose steel-keen edge could be blunted with sugar, milk, and other condiments too strange for Jory to name. He didn't care about the confusion of this wonderful new world whirling around his head--he was just glad to be alive. Then, as always, the thought of Ramy followed, and he felt a wrenching sadness.

That, in turn, reminded him of Girex and Giru. "Josenda, there is one thing," he said as she walked carefully juggling two small, white ceramic cups on tiny plates.

"Yes?" she asked attentively, since apparently it was her job to hover around him like a mother, a friend, and a police officer. She handed him his cup and they sat down. "Careful, it's hot," she said. He took his first sip of kjaba and spit it out. Not only was it hot, but it was sheer black hell.

"Ah!" he cried, handing her the cup and running to the sink. He heard clouds of laughter all around him as he rinsed his mouth out. "Sacred Oba Mountain, that stuff will kill you."

"You'll grow to like it," Josenda said.

Minutes later, sipping gingerly at a cup doused in condiments, he began to appreciate the cloying but robust way this drug entered his senses of smell and taste and made his blood run faster.

"There is one thing." He pictured Girex and Giru sprawled in their sad and dishonored deaths. "I had two friends here in Kusi-O. They were very gentle and took good care of me. I wish we could take them with us for burial. They have a child who will wonder what happened to them."

The three men howled with derision, and Jory almost hated them. He could see why the galaxy had rebelled against their human overlords hundreds of mendz ago--if the legends were true--.

Josenda seemed poised as ever, and he sensed resistance from her also. "Jory, it's impossible. The risks... the timing... the laws... we'd have to negotiate with the local authorities, and one thing would lead to another. Do you realize that if anyone learns about you, you'll be marked for death?" She set her cup aside and spoke firmly. "Maybe you don't understand. It's illegal for the five of us to exist on this planet. Or for that matter to run free in most of the galaxy. We have for centuries been under a shoot to kill edict. We don't own these ships or run this cargo. We have proxies and overlords like Captain Aptath."

"Captain Aptath isn't human?"

"Well... he is of our kind," she said slowly. "You'll learn more about this ship soon enough. The officers and the crew of the ship are Ruandap." She continued: "For us to make arrangements like this would involve Captain Aptath's officers contacting the Fril police and somehow explaining... no, it can't be done, I'm sorry."

Jerzy and company still laughed. "A couple of snake drug addicts, ho ho!"

Don slapped his sides. "Hope they don't clog up the incinerator."

Jory rose and walked close. "Gentlemen, if you amuse yourselves further, this will become very personal, very quickly. I warn you."

Their expressions faded into looks of disbelief and joshing. "Oh come on, man, we're just having a laugh."

"The Fril couple were kind to me. I would like to bury them with honor. Where I come from, we honor those who have died."

"But these are reptiles."

"No, they were people. They treated me like a person."

Hans rose huffily to refill his kjaba at the sink, and he brushed past Jory. He was a big man who moved in hulking movements, and Jory heard him mutter in his thick patois, "I can see why they would kill you on the other side." He shook his cup out on the floor and walked to the kjaba urn. "If I don't take you back there and toss you over the wall myself."

Josenda rose. "Hans, this man is worth a million of you to Captain Aptath. I will throw you over the wall if you even say another word."

"Keep your beans in the bag," Hans muttered.

Jory turned to her. "I insist that we make an effort."

"All right," she said, snapping open a com pad. " Dora Mora, this is Josenda. Patch me through to the O.D." She walked out of the room, slamming the door shut, leaving Jory with the men.

Jory stood his ground and looked at them.

Jerzy waved his arm. "It's not worth the sizzle. Ease up, O'Call. You made your *qif*in' point and I respect you for it. Don't push it by being rectal."

"I'm not pushing anything. I'm prepared to answer any further questions."

Hans scoffed to himself, but appeared to be thinking that the price of pursuing this wasn't worth it. They were human, on a hostile planet, and subject to execution if someone slipped up.

Don apologized. "Sorry, man. We all have buried dead. We know the feeling."

Jory slowly turned away from the confrontation, thinking, yes, and half of them you probably killed, being mercenaries.

Josenda re-entered the room. "Captain Aptath will send an officer to the Fril boss. He'll say that he was contacted by the child's guardians to retrieve his parents' bodies." She appeared somewhat surprised. "I can see you'll have your way around here." She remained friendly enough, but something had changed. Jory figured it out soon enough. He wasn't one of them. He was a special person whose any word to the Captain (whom he hadn't met yet, nor whose purpose he knew) could affect them in unknown ways. Suddenly it was the woman and the three mercenaries on one side of a wall, and Jory alone on the other.

When the bodies of Girex and Giru were brought to the boat hours later by Fril mortuary workers, Jory looked down from the secrecy of the curtained mezzanine office. He was alone in the room. Josenda had gone to freshen up after making sure the doors were securely locked, and the three mercenaries had gone to catch up on their sleep.

Jory felt sad, seeing naked Fril laborers carelessly handling the two yellow ceramic tubes smeared with black calligraphy. Then he spotted his first Ruandap. There were three of them, big men in uniforms similar to Josenda's, with side arms. One appeared to be a ship's officer, for he wore a colorful sash around his neck, and a gold medal on his chest. He had dark, blunt features. The Ruandap officer and a Fril representative nodded and shook hands. Fril workers carried the containers to a safe spot in the ship.

The boat lifted on time with a powerful whine of all four grav-desist engines, while Jory, Josenda, the mercenaries sat strapped into high-backed chairs in a passenger transit bay on the third floor. Josenda explained that the engines still had to push the boat upward, but somehow the engines fooled the atmosphere into thinking it was more like water and the ship more like a block of wood.

They rose into the night sky. He saw more stars as the atmosphere thinned and his field of vision deepened. The red moon showed its valleys and rilles.

The boat burned upward, and they seemed to move in several directions all at once, and always in shifting combinations, that made his stomach feel like a balloon full of air. Josenda slipped him a small bag just in time, and he expelled the last of Giru's vegetable soup, bless her soul. He rinsed with mint tea.

They slowed to a crawl before a huge black shape with myriad tiny squares of light in its many surfaces. Rockets fired in near-zero grav. The boat slowly bumped to a stop inside a featureless cage just big enough to hold it, and the boat was bolted to the floor and ceiling. Only then were the humans allowed to get out. Jory followed Josenda on shaky legs.

As they walked down the metal ramp, Jory looked around in amazement.

Josenda laughed at his expression. "It's big all right. But it's average. RTL runs hundreds of freighters up and down the Third

Arm. Some of them are so big the Dora Mora could fit into a single cargo bay."

Jory could not imagine that. He craned his neck as he walked. This was a noisy, industrial environment. There was room for four or five boats; at the moment, only one was out and he assumed still on the ground here or on Fril. The ceilings receded into darkness, and he could not see how high they went-- he was blinded by round factory lights that floated on cross-stabilizing cables. The ship had its own gravity, he noted, though he felt a little bit different, just a fraction--he couldn't tell if it was more or less gravity than on Shur.

They passed knots of humans in overalls. All were busy--some pushing cargo around on small gravdesist floats, others welding metal on metal so sparks flew before their black safety lenses, others trooping to the water cooler or carrying electric data tablets around.

Josenda took him up in a lift. "You'll stay in your own quarters on the Officers' Deck. What a lucky guy. I'll get to see you most of your waking hours though."

"When do I begin to find out why he brought me here?"

"When he's ready." She spoke deferently of the Ruandap.

"I will be patient." He waited in the dim light as the lift hummed.

When the lift stopped, they stepped into a pleasantly gloomy, wide corridor with carpeted floors and electronic lighting. The walls and doors were paneled in wood, and all the doors were closed, their heavy brass handles ornate.

"This is where you will stay for the time being," she said, throwing open a door. Jory stepped into an oppressively close, musty smelling room with no flavor or personality. "Like a tomb," she said lightly, "let's freshen it up." She flicked switches, and the lighting closed in--brighter wherever he walked, dimmer the farther away. A faint sigh of machinery caused delightful cool, fresh air to waft around Jory. A wall flickered into life, showing a panoramic sunset over a sea somewhere in the universe. The air, wherever that was, seemed to be on fire. "If you want music, entertainment, you have everything." She flicked some more switches, and music blared over him, and the wall changed to a scene of naked women strutting with feathered fans. She turned off the music, and the sunset returned. "Blast your senses numb after I'm gone if you wish."

"Thank you, I like the quiet."

She stood awkwardly and squeezed her hands together. "Maybe I should be direct, Jory. I am married, so don't get any ideas."

He felt his cheeks burn red. He'd already had some ideas, albeit dim and unrealized. He wanted to say something clever, but couldn't think of anything.

She showed him a refrigerator and a kitchen. He had a bathroom, whose workings she explained to him. "You know how to flush, yes?"

"How to what?"

"Flush." She pushed a button, and water swirled away, replaced by transparent fresh water colored blue like a mountain stream. "After you go. And always wash thoroughly afterward. It's important, because we're in confined quarters, and we have to keep the bugs under control."

After she bid him goodnight and left, he turned and looked into a mirror. He saw how different he looked. He tried cupping his palms over the round horn plates on his temples, but he still looked different. What human woman would want him?

He ate a few prepared foods with a spoon, not knowing how to hold them or what to put on them. He learned quickly that, no matter how a thing tasted, if in doubt, there was a small bottle of red liquid that would cover the food's smell and taste with a blanket of fire as potent as those flaming sunsets roiling on the walls.

After eating, he lay on the bed and watched the wall. After a while, he figured out that there were controls in a side panel of the bed. He simply had to march his fingers up and down the edge of the bed. As he did so, the pictures changed. He was fascinated by markets and beaches and roads and waving life forms on various worlds. Before falling asleep, however, he gazed at a scene of women who wore tiny two-piece bathing suits and lingered around a square pool of greenish-blue water whose surface rippled in a hot white noon sun.

In the next few days, Jory received a thorough medical exam and was pronounced fit. He must eat more fruits and vegetables, he was told, and from then on, every day a new basket of such food arrived in his room.

Wearing undistinguished second-hand--but clean; around Josenda, always clean--overalls, he strolled the length and breadth of the ship, just on the two decks reserved for humans, and sampled its pleasures--restaurants, holo houses, wine shops. She took him to a viewing blister upside, where the unwavering stars spread out in motionless disarray.

After a few days, someone knocked at the door, and Jory yelled "Come!" thinking it was Josenda. But, as the door drifted open, in the hall stood three persons like himself. Jory jumped up from his bed, startled. One was a tall, broad-shouldered older man with white wavy hair and a handsome if florid face wrinkled with too many *kjirs*--Malinu.

The second was a shorter, slighter man, much younger, with the slitted eyes Jory had seen in Don--Kinkidai.

The third was a woman--skinny, small, cold--Nolani. She had almond eyes like Josenda, but her skin was white and waxy.

All three wore plush brown overalls with no marks of wear on them. Also, all three had keratin plates on the sides of their heads as Jory did.

"May we come in?" Malinu asked after introducing the three. He had a pleasant, modulated voice.

"Of course," Jory said. He showed them to the corner table, which had four chairs.

Malinu said: "We are astropaths. I take it you are one of us, or will be shortly."

"That's the first I've heard. Sorry I have nothing to serve you."

"It's all right. We can order something later. Maybe a hot kjaba?"

"With lots of condiments," Jory replied. Malinu appeared charmed, Kinkidai calmly nodded with a certain reservation, and Nolani merely opened her dark eyes wider as if he'd said something shocking. Nolani puzzled Jory. He studied the black makeup around her eyes, the perfect little silver bowtie in her forehead, the rings in her cheeks, the way her long black hair was wound in braids to make a crown atop her head.

While Kinkidai raised a wrist gadget to his ear and spoke softly to the ship's galley, Malinu said: "The Captain will meet with you this evening, and he wanted us to explain the rudiments of our work to you. Have you ever traveled in space before?"

Jory shook his head.

"I can see we must start at the beginning. Have you seen the observation deck?"

"Yes. Josenda took me there and I had a long look. It's boring in a way, and yet very impressive."

"It will be more impressive when I tell you some numbers related to what you are looking at. We'll go there later."

"Are you the only three Astropaths on this ship?" Jory asked Kinkidai.

"Yes."

"Are we fairly rare in the universe then?"

Kinkidai had answered the real question already. For whatever reason, neither Malinu nor Kinkidai appeared to be possible partners for Nolani. Was it expected, then, that she pair with Jory? Such a rash assumption would explain why the woman looked so--scared, he could see now.

"We are one in tens of millions," Malinu said. "Millions of humans died when the aliens revolted against our kind centuries ago. Millions of us were shipped off into slavery. Your branch wound up as slaves on Shur, with the Obans. Judging by the size of your *keradz*, you may prove to have some prodigious talent. We'll know soon enough."

"So what is it, exactly, that I have a talent for?"

Malinu described their work. "Have you ever skipped a stone on a pond?"

Jory frowned. His childhood had been dark and without much play. His parents had not been very warm people, though they had fed him and comforted him when he was sick. A memory teased up, of playing by the river with several other human boys. "You mean, tossing a flat pebble with spin, like so"-- he imitated--"so that the pebble jumps out of the water several times before it falls in?"

"Exactly!" the other three said all at once.

Malinu continued: "That's how we get through long stretches of space. Plain ordinary motion at the speed of light is impossible, but we manage to skip outside of space, using a special hyper-light drive, and return, like the pebble, or like a frog hopping from stone to stone. The more closely we aim the pebble, and are able to plan its trajectory, the more efficient our travel becomes. That's where we come in. A sentient brain is still the most complex and finely honed tool in the universe. The old humans dickered around with their own genetic material. They did things you and I and most people alive today would not dare. But they were sure they were invincible, and that's what brought them down. They did many daring things, and one of them was to introduce a strain of genes into the race that would enable us astropaths to sharpen the trajectory of a ship through hyperspace by finer and finer degrees."

Under the observation blister, Kinkidai explained while Malinu and Nolani leaned against the brass railing on either side. "We are in the Third Arm of our galaxy, which is an average size galaxy that has two smaller companion galaxies, one of them twice the size of the other. According to legend, somewhere in this Arm or maybe the next lies a planet called Earth, which was our original home as a kind, but most people nowadays think Earth was a myth. The aliens scoff at us and say we invented Earth to make ourselves feel important. They say we are a kind of roach that grows naturally in any dark place."

"Do you believe in Earth?" Jory asked.

The three remained silent. Kinkidai cleared his throat. "Let the Captain speak about that this evening." He told Jory how far away things were. He pointed to a star that seemed just two rooms away and said: "If you travel at half the speed of light, it will take you a million kjirs--twelve million mendz--to get there."

Jory grew quiet as they squashed him with statistical monstrosities, one more absurd than the other.

Next, they went to their place of work in a protruding nodule in the lower human deck. Jory noticed that, as they approached the busier parts of the ship, people parted the way for them and nodded distantly, without warmth. They got many strange stares. Malinu said: "We are freaks to them. They can consort with all sorts of aliens much stranger looking than we are, but they are revolted at the sight of one of their own with plates on the head like a lizard."

They passed through the industrial areas and into quiet, plushly carpeted corridors that were indirectly lit. Malinu said: "They do treat us well, even if at arms' length. They know we need to concentrate, so they carpet our halls and keep the lights dim. This is our part of the ship, Jory. This is Astropathy. I'm the First Astropath, which is like a ship's first officer, only a hair's rank below. Kinkidai is Second Astropath, and Nolani is Third Astropath."

"Would I theoretically be Fourth Astropath?" Jory almost laughed. "I'd have nobody to give orders to below me."

"On the contrary," Kinkidai said, "we rank just under the top officers, who are all Ruandap; but, other than that, we are outside the chain of command. Their lives depend on us, because we can get them where they want to go in half the time, but if we make a mistake, we can all land in the heart of some sun. You can imagine how long we'd last. They may not like our looks but they have deep respect for us, and even fear."

"Outside the chain of command?" Jory asked, bemused.

"Yes," Malinu said. His face darkened. "Humans are supposed to be slaves. They can't be ship's officers." "That's why you'll find service aboard the Dora Mora to be very exceptional. We keep the secret among ourselves and move from port to port before rumor can follow. Our masters are--well, you'll see."

They passed through a spacious offices revolving on a blister deck, all unmanned and dark except for the surrounding starlight. They entered a huge bubble further on, whose ceiling was glassix-like the blister on the ob deck, and again Jory saw the fields upon fields of stars.

Six comfortable captain's chairs occupied the central area of the floor. Though there were instrument panels around the periphery of this room that looked as though it could hold twenty people, the chairs were unadorned.

"Sit here," Malinu ordered. As Jory sat back in the comfortable chair, Kinkidai said: "Relax. We're going to hook you up and you'll get your first feel of this."

"We're between jumps right now," Malinu explained, "or all three of us would be strapped in here, working together. It will be a wonderful addition to have your power, if it is as considerable as we think it may be."

Nolani put a kind of well-padded, comfortable cotton helmet on. Its foam interior molded automatically to the exact shape of her skull, leaving the area of her keradz exposed. As he lay looking up, Jory saw the array of cables and fasteners hanging on retractable trapezes over each of the six chairs. Nolani lowered his trapeze. She and Kinkidai began doing thing to his keradz, and he squirmed as it tickled. He'd never had any use for the things, and wished he could pull them out of his head.

"I'm going to power up," Malinu said. "Let me know when you see or feel anything."

Kinkidai placed a pair of black goggles over Jory's eyes that made him blinder than a human on Oba Island. Jory felt a hum of power, and then saw tiny red and amber lights wink on in the goggles. "I see little red lights."

"Good. That's the beginning of the metaphor. Keep looking, and relax. This is a live run, but there's nothing you can do to alter course or cause any harm."

"Tomorrow we will begin a live session as we prepare for the next jump," Malinu said. "See anything more?"

Jory's field of vision expanded as a host of white and red lines started to appear. The lines raced across the field, vertically and horizontally, chasing each other and blurry speeds, while tiny yellow and blue globes slid along the lines this way and that. Jory cried out and tore the goggles off.

"Blink next time," Kinkidai said. "Close your eyes and will it under control. You must find that on your own. You must bring it under control or your gift isn't much use."

"Relax," Nolani said. She stood with her arms crossed around herself, as if she wanted to be an island from him.

He put his goggles back on and lay back. The lines appeared, and he squinted. They appeared to break up, crumble into dust, disappear--then they appeared again. He practiced making them go away by squinting. "I still have no idea what this is all about," he noted. "But the squinting helps."

"They go away and reappear?" Malinu asked anxiously.

"Yes."

Malinu shook Jory's shoulder in congratulations.

"Then you have a powerful gift," Kinkidai said.

Freshly barbered, and wearing overalls, Jory appeared at the Captain's door, escorted by Josenda. She knocked, and, when a small light winked above, pushed the door open for him. "Good luck, Jory. I'll be on call when you're done."

Jory stepped into a sprawling, low-ceilinged, carpeted space that reeked of luxury. Josenda pulled the door shut behind him.

"This way!" a rich voice boomed.

Jory, noting the paintings and sculptures all around, abstract and mute, followed the sound of the voice around a wallpapered corner. A wide flight of stairs, three shallow steps deep, brought him down into a lower dining room. Carpeted stairs cascaded up in three directions to more carpeted acreage--one a library, another a working office with desk laden with electronic tablets, the third a casual lounge.

"Welcome," boomed the huge man who sat at the central place of honor. He had a dark mane of hair, and short black hair fairly bursting from his white blouse. He appeared to have taken off his leather uniform, for he swaggered about in cloth breeches that reached just below the knee. "I'm Captain Aptath N'Ruandap. You recognize my other guest?" Aptath nodded to a man who stepped out of the shadows.

A bald man of indeterminate age, the man wore an expensive black uniform with fine silver piping. "Colonel Jstraki at your service, Astropath." He bowed slightly. "We met before."

Jory suddenly recognized him. "Yafi of Anamo, outside Kusi-O!" Jory was too surprised to be angry at the scoundrel who'd seemed to have handed him to the Imperial road police.

Aptath, as he filled two glasses from a bottle, said: "Colonel Jstraki is a skilled agent for Ruandap Intelligence. When I headed for the Shur system, rumor of your existence floated by me. I couldn't resist the temptation to find you and commission you. It took an agent of Jstraki's caliber a kjir to worm his way in, invent a local personality--"

"--In that infernal dampness and gloom!--" Jstraki injected.

"--Find you, and bring you out."

Jory remembered nothing of the period from when he saw Yafi receiving payment from the Obayyo police official until he woke up sick as a dog in Girex and Giru's chimney. "How did you manage to smuggle me through the drum wall?"

Jstraki grinned coldly, evidencing ferocious intelligence and efficiency. "We have two old sayings on Ruandap--Gravity is heavy no matter where you are in the universe. I found the cracks in the system very easily. Also: Money penetrates all, like water finding its way through a crack. I paid the right people, and, I'm afraid to admit, killed a few others. We wrapped you up in a membrane with state of the art AIC breathing apparatus, knocked out colder than a day-old noodle, and secreted you in a vat of fungus."

"I thought I was poisoned by the babas," Jory said. He remembered the taste and wanted to spit, but only made a bitter face.

"No," Jstraki said, "I didn't need to rely on native crafts. The drug was JF-VII, and I almost feared we had lost you at one point. I think Giru's soup brought you back to life."

"They were good people," Jory said stubbornly.

Jstraki laughed coldly and shook Jory's hand. "A man of principle. I leave you now."

Aptath handed Jory a glass and raised his own in a toast. "I celebrate the arrival of a promising astropath."

Jory stared into his glass. "No more kjaba surprises?"

Aptath laughed. "It's wine, a drink they used to make on Earth from a fruit called the grape."

Jory sipped. The liquid was dry, and made him sweat. Its taste had a strangely robust, rubbed quality, like something overripe and too sweet, but also severe. It had many interesting after tastes that lingered like broken music notes.

"Have a seat," Aptath boomed.

Jory chose the casual lounge, walking up to a circle of C-shaped couches around a central glass table at knee height. Surrounding them was a bubble, and outside that were the stars.

Aptath sat down opposite. "Welcome aboard. How do you like it so far?"

"I could be dead in an Oba latrine."

"So it's upward of that?" Aptath said patiently as he refilled the two plain, transparent glasses that had narrow glass stems and a wider glass foot.

"I must measure all things from there, Sir; forgive me, I didn't mean to seem rude."

"No offense taken, young man." He handed Jory the half-empty bottle with a paper label on it. "Recognize that?"

Jory stared at the label, at the bottom of the bottle, into the neck. He sniffed the liquid, which was yellowish and smelled musty-sweet.

"That's white wine," Aptath said. "Of course, I forget your people on Shur have been cut off for centuries." He sat back and sipped his wine. "We're only beginning, Jory. We haven't even started to turn the tide. But we'll win the galaxy back."

"We, Captain?"

"We--yes." He slipped into near-reverie. "We from Earth."

"You believe in those legends?"

Aptath smiled. "Oh yes." His eyes glowed as if he were looking directly at the mythical planet. "I have seen it with my own eyes, so close and so pretty that it seemed I could reach out and hold it in my two hands." He held up his hands and looked from one hand to the other. "But our ship could go no closer. No closer than Earth's single stony, battered moon. A big moon it is, that shines greenish, with an odd sort of pattern in the light, like a man singing."

Jory listened to this recitation and wondered if the man were mad, or drunk. But his voice wasn't slurry, and his manner was steady.

"It was the most glorious run of my life, and one day I must do it again, not once but a thousand times. You should stay with us, Jory O'Call, you have the gift of planets and stars in your blood. We can make a run there again. She's round, and blue as ice, with white clouds around her like angel dust. She is a fine confection, mostly ocean, but with deep swatches of green forest and mountain ranges that sing in the wind, I'm told."

Jory swallowed, then spoke slowly, "You say you've been to--Earth?"

"Yes." Aptath's eyes still glowed. "It's a secret only a few of us know. Only a few of us on this ship, including the Astropaths."

"Where is it?"

"That's the rub, Jory. I don't know. It's a secret. We'll have to look for her. When the old Earth empire fell, the last pre-Inversion scientists hid her in a well of time. They were powerful people, your race. Our kind. They did many things. Why do you think you carry those horn plates in your skull?"

"They cultured some of their own kind to specialize--?"

"Yes. They had no regard for the individual."

Jory was silent, thinking about the cruelties of Oba--and now, apparently, the whole galaxy.

"Do you know," Aptath said thickly, "at one time your race hunted my race?"

Jory shook his head slowly. "The old women who count mendz don't tell such stories. Much is lost."

"Ah, not lost, just misplaced, like Earth herself."

Jory said: "Why do you say 'your race' in one breath and 'our kind' in the next?"

"Because both our races come from Earth. Any living thing from Earth is our kind, Jory, though we may be a million races and species. Even those of us who were altered, like you and I."

Jory frowned. "You are--?"

Aptath set his wine glass aside and rose. "Let's see if you have any racial memory at all." He reared up to his full height. "Does this strike any chords in you?" He took off his shirt, revealing a brawny, furry body twice the size of the largest human man's. He held his arms out as far as he could, as if extending something flexible. Then he curled his hands inward, leaned forward stiff-backed, and, touching his fists to the table top, leaned massively on his knuckles. "My legs are longer than they should be, and my arms are a bit shorter so that I can walk more like you. Before they altered us a bit, they came to hunt us. Some of your race protected us, but many of my race were killed for their hands and feet, which some of your race ignorantly believed could be made into medicine. For that alone, I should kill all of you. But then, you gave us some of the spark from the fire of your own intelligence. I like to think we have used it more wisely. Do you recognize me, Jory boy?"

Jory shook his head slowly, as if the Captain's words had made him drunk with their heaviness.

"I am a gorilla."

The room steeped in silence for a moment, while they stood frozen--the man, an underling, sitting uncomfortably on the edge of his couch, while the gorilla, a space captain, demonstrated a posture that was but a memory.

Aptath broke the spell by walking quickly to a small book case and bringing back two pictures. Each showed a hairy creature whose face resembled Aptath's, in a posture much like the one Aptath had just demonstrated. "Here is one of my ancestors long ago. The other is yours."

While Jory studied the picture, Aptath poured the rest of the wine.

"Is this somewhere on Earth then," Jory asked.

"Yes. It's on the savannah in a place called Africa. A place called Rwanda, to be specific, in a rain forest where my race lived for millions of kjirs before--all hell broke loose." He held up the bottle. "This wine, Jory, is from Earth. I was very young, and our captain was an alien, a scoundrel. He was accepted for the secret trade route, but he tried to sell the secret, and their spies killed him in the next port before he could pry the first word through his teeth. Our spies, I should say. We are still a dangerous kind."

Jory said: "I never had a choice about being born on Oba of Shur. I never had a chance to decide when my parents sold me to the palace. I never did choose my way out. But here I am, and I could say no?"

"Most assuredly," Aptath said darkly.

"Then I freely say yes."

"Good!" Aptath boomed, reaching for Jory's hand. "Welcome to my crew. I make you Astropath Four, but I think you will rise to the top of your profession. Let those three teach you what you need to know. You'll be safe with me. I've been sailing for fifty kjirs, and I've never once lost a single human crew member to the alien terror. The Inversion of Man, I should say. And of you I will take special care, for you will be the sail that takes me down the well of time and to that wonderful blue vision once more." He held up his glass. "It was one of my last bottles. I managed to buy a case of them, shipped up from a place called San Francisco."

They clinked glasses.

Aptath spoke softly. "You know what decided me on you? You know what made me want to trust you with this information? It was the way you insisted on a proper burial for those two Fril people. The child will be very sad, but it is expected he will live despite his sickness, and at least he will be able to visit their grave. You are an honorable man, Jory O'Call. You are a fine human. I will enjoy working with you."

Jory said "Thank you." He waggled his near-empty glass. "Time to go back for more." He sipped the last few mouthfuls tenderly, savoring every molecule. "I think I can taste Earth. I can taste real sunshine."

Jory learned the trade of an Astropath. Soon enough, as they prepared for the next skip on the surface of space and time, Malinu and Kinkidai and Nolani invited him for the first time to help. Together, they steered through the critical interstices that could either throw them into some forever loop where they would die, or skip them through a tight, efficient course to the next point on the invisible surface. In their virtual world, the black goggles made their path a tunnel of fine, light circles. Everything was a metaphor--the ship, the surface, the contact point, the trajectory. At first, everything happened too quickly for Jory to comprehend. He gripped the arm rests and hung on as he seemed to flash at breakneck speed toward the uniformly charcoal-gray surface. As he drew near, the surface took on characteristics--bumps, ripples, hooks, holes, all mathematical artifacts that said, essentially, 'if you touch here, you blow up.' Each type of characteristic had its own meaning, which the astropaths instantly recognized and for which they knew how to compensate.

The ship was a red quadrille that fled over this landscape. What looked like a red grid-echo rippling over the surface distortions was not a shadow thrown behind, but a projection moving ahead--'if you go near here, sense or calculate what will happen.' Vertical blue lines converged with horizontal green lines at rapid speed, often faster than the eye could follow. The astropaths were able to take all these variables and, in the power grid of their brains between their keradz plates, arrange them tighter and tighter as the ship approached the critical Skip Step, until the ship was once again headed out on a new trajectory. Malinu told Jory: "It's like running a race. You have to bring a ball to the other end, but you may not carry the ball. You have to keep hitting the ball with a paddle so it arcs up, then down again, where you hit it back up. That's very difficult to do, say for several klix. Imagine how easy it would be to hit the ball on a wrong trajectory. If it drops once, you lose. The rules are kind of like that here, only the price of losing is death for all of us."

While he learned astropathy, Jory also began to understand how far his intellectual and social skills were removed from those of his fellow humans on the ship. Nobody here was interested in the court game of putting together strings of two or three line poems in ancient Oban. Many of these humans conversed on a level far below his, and yet he felt belittled and isolated. He didn't understand a thousand of their nuances, glances, small gestures, grunted syllables for this or that.

In his isolation, he fit in (reluctantly) with the other three astropaths. All three were unmarried. Malinu and Kinkidai were friends who liked to play casta, an ancient game with a 64-square board and two opposing armies of little wooden pieces including a king and a queen. They sometimes also played a 512-square variation that had 8 levels instead of one. For social life, the two men would visit Long Street, a pleasure district in any ship. The Dora Mora's Long Street was a block long and had six places to take a limited variety of mild recreational drugs, like alcohol. One place was for women only, another for men only, and the rest for various gender combinations.

Several times, Jory accompanied Malinu and Kinkidai to these bars. Jory enjoyed the drinks, and the women were delightful to look at, but astropaths were hardly sex symbols, and the women shrugged them off. After a while, Jory grew tired of these places. He began to long for the journey to be over so he could set foot on planetary soil somewhere, and he knew that was a bad attitude for an astropath. Given his deformity, that was really the life he'd been designed for. Maybe someplace a surgeon could be found who'd cut these things out of his skull and repair his brain. Malinu shook his head when Jory voiced the thought one night, and Malinu said: "You can't escape it. It's you, and it would kill you if they took this gift from your brain. Our ancestors were ruthless."

Then Jory had an affair with Nolani. It began one night when Jory, Nolani, and the two male astropaths were walking home from work. Malinu and Kinkidai wanted to go to Long Street. Jory thanked them and said he'd rather not. Nolani offered to walk home with him while the other two left.

Nolani was his height, but thin, with shiny black hair. Her skin was pale as a riverbank mushroom on Oba. He was lonely, and he suspected she was too. There was a special glow about her skin as they walked slowly, talking about everything and nothing, about music and space and small pets. He kept looking at the skin on her arms, seeing every tiny hair, every spot and blemish. He noticed for the first time that she affected a bracelet made of several colored threads twined into one. Suddenly he became aware that, under those loose overalls, walked a female form with soft spots and swaying parts that were designed to arouse him.

They walked on the long alley on the outer side of the human work deck until they had gone all the way around the ship. Then they climbed up a deck and walked around the ship a second time. Here and there they passed pseudo-windows that picked up light on the outer skin of the ship and transmitted the light through the ship's hull, to be reassembled as a picture on the inner surface. At other times, they passed small shops with glowing neon signs. They passed one or two bars where women's hard laughter poured out.

Then, because there was really no place else to go, they came to her quarters and she let him in. She served icy beer. They sat in her sunken living room and watched a funny motion picture in which the hero and heroine kissed often. The hero had to rescue the heroine from her silly attraction to a handsome charmer who was actually after her money.

Somewhere during the second half of the picture, Jory slid closer on the couch to Nolani. She did not move away. He put his arm around the area behind her back, and she stayed put. He could see the frozen way she held herself, the way her eyes grew wide and her mouth dry as she stared at the big screen. He settled back and lightly pulled her by the shoulders. She settled against his side, her hands and head on his chest. She was surprisingly light and dainty. After a time, he grasped her shoulders with the lightest of touches and guided her to him so that they kissed. Her tongue was surprisingly firm and hungry. She rose and dropped the overalls around her feet so that she wore only flimsy undergarments; her breasts were small and needed no support. He touched her legs, admiring the sheen of her skin in the flickering colored lights of the movie. She turned slightly, and he found himself looking toward the flickering light source between her legs. Thoroughly aroused, he took her hips, gently, and pulled her toward him. She knelt down and undid his overalls and pulled them off, down his legs. Then she explored him with her fingers and lips. The screen went dead except for a silent and unending stream of reddish light particles, not unlike on a journey through space, while Jory and Naloni had sex on the couch. She was slight but strong. She was passionate, but in a noncommittal way that lessened his pleasure slightly. He felt relieved and pleasured and at ease afterward, and would have fallen asleep, but she insisted he go to his quarters. This baffled him a bit, but he staggered home and fell asleep alone in his bed.

They spent several evenings together, always with that long walk, and then the movie ritual, followed by sex, and then his return home alone. While he enjoyed her in a limited way, Jory began to sense an emptiness about his affair with her. It was going nowhere, and neither of them really wanted it to. He supposed she must see him as a rude ex-slave from the island of Oba on the moon Shur. In his turn, he simply did not see in her the qualities that would attract him--as Ramy, for instance, had.

Jory busied himself as much as possible with catching up on the school learning he'd missed--and it was frustrating because he had almost no foundation. Had he been a mere riverbank nah on Oba, there would be no hope for him. Because he did live in a castle, and could recite from memory the entire canon of Oban literature in Classic, Middle Period, and Modern forms, he did have a foundation of discipline and memorizing. Gradually, as the mendz flashed by, he surpassed Nolani at astropathy. His school learning began to grow close in some areas to the learning of the humans raised on Ruandap.

Jory found a cap he could wear, a wool cap designed for cold planet air, and its ear flaps coincidentally also covered his keradz. He began to visit the library and any social events he could find himself invited to. Gradually, he built a small, loose circle of acquaintances around a club whose members did strenuous cycling and jogging in the Dora Mora's inner gravity mill. He found it very difficult to penetrate their social sphere. The men were distant, the women generally cold. This began to change as one of the more attractive women invited herself along with Jory on a group walk. The woman's name was Ohella. She was a slim, perky brunette with a blunt freckled nose and a sassy mouth. She was an apprentice machinist on the factory floor, and had rough hands to show for it. She introduced him to the ship's human swimming pool, which was a revelation to Jory. He loved the water. She taught him swimming, and, after a light supper and a glass of wine at her place, how to do 'go around the world.'

While he was seeing Ohella, Jory fortuitously learned that Nolani had been involved in a long-term affair with Malinu, who, because he was much older, let her play around on the side. Just as Jory turned off to Nolani, Ohella stopped seeing him.

Another young woman appeared in Ohella's place--Katjina, a blonde with limp, straight hair that gleamed like gold foil. She had strong thighs and a flat stomach. Her small, round breasts, slightly pendulous, were the only soft spots on her limbs or torso--except of course her wet place that she took him to explore.

After a while, Katjina seemed to find a boyfriend-- who, oddly, had been there all along--and it was Moryah's turn. She was small and dark-skinned, like Josenda, and had a full figure that did not display much energy. She quickly went away, replaced by another, and another.

This life became more and more empty for Jory. He could not seem to go below the surface with any of these people. The women would have sex for a few weeks and drift on. For a long time, he thought that was how they lived. Then he began to notice that one or another of the women took up with the same boyfriends they'd had before. The men tended to be cold toward him, and gradually he dropped out of his clubs one by one, until the library was his only social life. Even there, he found women to take to bed. In his heart, he only wished to find one he could love with the same deep affection he'd had for his Ramy. But there would never be another Ramy, nor for that matter another Oba, or Shur, or childhood as a castle pet.

One day, as he lay in his quarters reading, came a knock on the door. He rose, slipped on his wool cap, and opened. Josenda stood outside, wearing a dark blue off-duty jump suit. "Hello," she said with a smile as startled as his, "I haven't seen you in a while, so I thought I would check up on you." She seemed nervous or something.

"Come in." He let her in and closed the door.

"This is a nice place." Something was wrong.

"Thank you." He wondered what it was.

"Can I sit down?"

"Sure." He folded up the unmade bed so it became a couch. He went into the kitchen to heat water for tea. "How have you been?"

She seemed to deflect his question as she sat down on the couch and rubbed her hands together as if creating sparks for a fire. "So! What passes in your life?"

It took but a minim for the water to boil. "Lemon or *kivi*?"

"Plain."

"How unexciting." He brought two teas--both plain--and handed her one. Then he sat down in an easy chair nearby. "Are you well?" The conversation seemed to go in circles.

"Well," she said biting her lower lip, "yes. I'm going to be changing ships. We're going to arrive at Kandor 3c in another month, and I--well, I'll be leaving the ship."

"For another ship?"

"Yes. I will be on another ship."

"And your husband?"

"He'll--he'll be on another ship. Tell me, how's the astropath game?"

"I've learned many remarkable things," he said. He felt sad that she seemed to have broken up with her husband. He felt at ease with her, like an old friend. He took the cap off and laid it aside. "I've become more and more like you people, and yet these big ugly calluses will always make me different."

"Is there a woman in your life yet?"

"There have been some, but they seem to leave soon. Am I rude somehow?" He leaned forward anxiously. "Josenda, tell me honestly. What is it? I sense the men hate me, and the women seem to want me for a time, but then--well, I can't quite figure it out. Maybe you'll help me."

She rose and walked toward him. "Sure. I'll help you, but there's really nothing to help. You're fine the way you are. Maybe you are just too sensitive."

"That might be it," Jory said dubiously.

She took his hands in hers and pulled him up. "Why don't we just go out and have a drink and loosen up? It seems depressing in here."

"Oh, all right," he said cheerfully.

At the door, she turned ironically. "Aren't you forgetting something?"

He followed her gaze to the bed, and there lay his cap. "Oh, the cap! Yes!" He put it on. "With you, I'm so relaxed I forgot about it. Don't want strangers to stare, do we?"

They walked to the lift, rode down to the human work deck, and found a tiny corner snack stand. It was always night here in the factory womb of the ship, where workers toiled to keep the ship's parts repaired, and made manufactured goods from raw materials picked up along the ship's travels.

"I don't have much time," Josenda said, using traditional wooden sticks to slurp down noodles. She grabbed quick sips of her white wine. Jory nursed a dark beer. For the first time, she was being really friendly, and yet somehow it didn't wash with him.

They made small talk, and he found her steering him back to his place. As they entered, she said: "I'll bet you never guessed that I'm a trained masseuse."

"I would not have guessed."

"I'm going to run the hot water for a bath. Go get undressed and come when I tell you to."

He watched her walk away into his bathroom. He waited, motionlessly.

"Okay!" she called.

He walked slowly into the bathroom. For a moment, he was blinded by steam.

She had stripped off her clothing and left it on a chair. She wore a white terris towel that covered her breasts and torso. Her black curly hair glistened with swarms of tiny water droplets. She looked surprised. "I said to drop your clothes."

"Josenda," he said, advancing on her, "you're not separating from your husband, are you?"

"What do you mean, Jory. Don't look at me that way."

"I'm not looking at you any way. I have no argument with you. I am being treated like some sort of--of--farm animal by all of you." He saw himself as a fuzzy outline in a foggy mirror, but that alone was enough. He tore the wool cap off. "I'm a fool. People are laughing behind my back. The women want my sperm--why?"

"Darling."

"Don't--."

She held up her hands in a stop-motion. "All right. Jory, we're coming into port, and some of us are moving on. Do you know what it's worth to have a child like you? Captain Aptath would pay a fortune. He would raise you in the best of care, educate you, feed you--."

"That's already been done to me once, Josenda. I was sold by my parents. I lived in a castle. You would have been a river rat or worse, but I would have ridden by in a carriage with my mistress. I can recite the hundred lays of Mogi-Noro, a thousand kjir old series of children's stories, but I myself never had a childhood. Is that what you want for your child?"

She hung her head. "I was hoping you would understand. Meikol and I--my husband--we would raise the child ourselves. It's not like you think. Here the parents stay with a special child. Your child would get everything in the world, including our love and devotion."

Jory picked up her clothes and threw them into her arms. "Get out of here. You people make me sick. I am a freak, but you want a child by me who will be equally a freak. You lie in my face. Maybe you lie to yourself too, but how could you love a child who looks like me?"

"Please."

"No. Get out. Go be ashamed if you have the capacity to."

In his anger, he didn't wait for her to leave, but went out to his kitchen. His fingers shook as he tore off a piece of bread to chew nervously. He heard her rustling in the livingroom. He did not want to see her naked, for fear he would weaken.

"Goodbye, Jory." She seemed to wait.

"Go away."

He heard her rustle into her clothing. Then he heard the door open and shut. She'd left the towel thrown on the living room floor. He rushed and locked the door. This was worse than being on Oba, he thought as he sagged against the door. Only these were not Shurians--these were his own people. Or his own kind. Perhaps they were no more his people than were the Ruandap, though they were all one kind-- from Earth.

Jory worked harder than ever. He came to accept the detente between Malinu and Nolani, but he did not sleep with her again. That kept Malinu cordial, and put Nolani at ease, because she had tired of Jory and did not want to juggle more than one relationship.

Jory guessed she'd gone through a similar gyration with Kinkidai, but didn't ask.

Jory was now almost as good as Kinkidai, who was still a journeyman. The three of them fed off the experience and enormous talent of Malinu. Malinu, however, predicted that in ten kjirs, nobody would be able to match Jory.

Landfall came and went. Josenda and her husband disappeared. Kinkidai left the crew for another ship, and was replaced by a quiet, hard, dark-skinned man with narrow eyes, named Kawlin. Kawlin was thoroughly professional, but kept to himself otherwise, and Malinu said he missed Kinkidai's youthful company. Jory took up visits to the bars with Malinu to console him.

Jory began to have dreams of Oba.

He would wake up in the middle of the night and pace the ship's corridors. He had to force himself to be attentive at work. He quarreled with Malinu and Nolani, then with the new astropath.

And he dreamed of Ramy, his long-lost love.

…A day or two, after Lord Dumonhi had struck Ramy, and after the Lord had stormed out of her chambers, Jory happened to be on the glazed blue-tile roof, hiding just out of arms' reach. He heard some of Dumonhi's drunken retainers in the alleys between tile roofs and brick walls, and could not hide before they spotted him. These warriors were not so tolerant of a castle human, and two drew their swords to part Jory from his head. Their senior man restrained them, saying: "We are guests in this sacred house. We must not shed blood in the Lord Ramyon's house, even if this thing is a monkey." So they strode off, and Jory, who had not expected the confrontation, breathed a sigh of relief, thankful to be alive.

Hearing the clatter of shod hooves galloping away into the night, Jory crept, as quietly as a melting candle, up the familiar stairs. From a middle landing, heard her sobs. She cried continuously and heartbrokenly, each attack followed immediately by the next.

Pure instinct based on a lifetime of intimacy, trust, and affection made Jory knock on her door. He'd had many human girls, but they always soon left him because of the disfiguring horn plates inset in his temples. Ramy was the one female who'd been in his life since childhood, whom he could almost say he loved in a pure manner.

Ramy sat on the hard floor and cried bitterly. The door was ajar, and Jory let himself in, then slipped the lock shut.

She sat on the floor, where Dumonhi had left her. She pouted, full dark lips and radiant cheeks. She had blackened her teeth, as was the custom for beauty.

Now, her gray eyes stormed with pain and sorrow. She was so pale, by nature, that Jory could see blood pulsing, criss-crossed in blue-black veins, finer than spider's webs, under her nearly translucent skin. He compared her skin with pale seashells, warmed by the faintest of rose tinges here and there, yet cooled by the faintest of dawn blues there and here.

Her russet hair made a bright, large halo around her head, colored in the 99 shades of autumn sadness and joy.

From where this Shurian myth of hair, apples, and autumn stemmed on dark Oba, nobody remembered. Somewhere in the distant past were many deep secrets. But Oba and its secrets were not to be parted, for she was the fungal treasure chamber of the known universe. Her lords and merchants and priests guarded many secrets, none to tell, for their wealth and power were ancient, and buried in secrets.

The annual ritual of Harvest Thanks was also the occasion for weddings. The Silently Welcoming Tower and Gate ceremony required great patience, as a young couple sat facing each other from divans on opposite sides of their soon-to-be bed together, while her Baba hovered in the shadows outside.

Ramy had been destined for the throne beside a young lord to one day be great. Instead, she had been overpowered by intoxicant love, and had opened her robe to a slave. What might have been remained like a wistful hint of long-ago fragrance among death's silent marble walls.

Of pleasant marriage ceremonies, the ancient poet long ago keened in a well-textured voice, while a *kthara* twanged discrete notes each like a falling leaf, and hidden players tapped their instruments *bengo* and *mengo*, whose halting click-beat echoed in the hall as delicately as moonlight rises from lacquered surfaces:

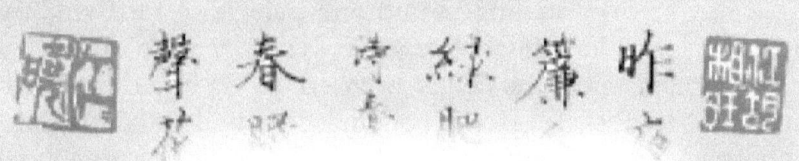

Beautiful woman seduces
with her black smile
and autumn-apple hair.
She loosens one end of her
belt from its chaste knot
and drops it by custom.
A man's heart stops, and
does not beat again
until she lays aside
the other end of her belt
so a pale moon at last
lights his shadowed sky.
If she waits a beat too
long, in all innocence,
feeling shamed or shy, or
wants to prolong his joy, a
girl may kill her lover.
He dies on his knees,
glimpsing heaven.

Ramy's dark, pouting mouth and pale nose bled slightly, and she hardly gave Jory any notice as he went to wet a cloth.

Returning to her, he gently brushed drying blood from her chin, her lips, her nostrils. Her blood indeed smelled faintly like late-summer apples ripening beyond their season. She let him touch her. They had grown up together from childhood, and were used to each other. She sniffled residually, with an occasional hiccup. Then she embraced him, as one would a stuffed animal. He was her comfort. He still held the wet cloth, which he dropped on the floor as he embraced her in turn.

They held each other, enjoying the gentle pleasure. He helped her up and walked her to her bed. It was a large bed, with four posts and an overhanging cloth. They had slept together many kjirs ago as child and pet. He helped her up and, as she lay back sighing, with one forearm draped over her forehead, he pulled the coverlet up over her fully clad form. She took his hand and pulled him to a seated position beside her. He sat on the bed for a long time, holding her hand, neither saying anything until he was sure she had fallen asleep. He admired the beauty of her features; in the half-light, she seemed more human than many women of Jory's kind. The reddish hair floated above the lovely mask of her face. When he grew tired and cramped, Jory sought to rise. As he began to gently disengage her hand from hers, she tightened her grip and pulled. She was not as strong as he, but he felt tender toward her. She opened the coverlet for him, as she might have ten kjirs earlier, and he slipped in beside her, still fully clothed.

They lay together, basking in one another's warmth. They nuzzled cheek to cheek, nose against neck, the arm of one around the chest of the other, and prepared to fall asleep. Yet the warmth and the scent of her hair and the feeling of her firm thighs caused something else. He heard the hard, deep breaths that signaled arousal. The whole world fell away--what the humans might say, what the Shurians might say--and they were two souls contained in a world of their own. They were on the brink of the unthinkable, even in their own thoughts-- but those thoughts were gone now, in the throes of ardor.

To better touch each other, they stripped their clothes off, one stroke of the hand at a time, wriggling and breathing deeply. Pretty soon, their mouths met. From his life at the castle, Jory knew what would happen next. The Shurians' tongues were not only organs of taste, but of sexuality far greater than among humans, and of self-expression. First, Jory kissed her lips, which grew moist. Like a Shurian male, he lightly licked her lips, and their moistness grew. Soon, the tip of her blue tongue appeared. She lay on her back, eyes closed, breath splashing in and out of her extended nostrils. Jory licked her tongue and felt it gradually extend out, one finger's thickness at a time. He was aroused himself, and he was happy to please her, so he continued. He put his mouth on her tongue, containing what he could of it (it would not all fit into his mouth), and sucked gently, moving his head up and down. She began to moan. She pulled at him until he swung on top of her. He was afraid to put his weight on her, but she pulled him down with surprisingly strong arms. All the while, he continued to suck on her tongue, which grew as stiff as it was slippery. The Shurians' single excretory organ was where the humans had their anus. The Shurians' male/female reproductive organs were midway on their bellies. Jory's member was erect and hard. He let her little fumbling fingers guide her to the indentation in her belly that was already soaked with her lubricants. He slipped inside easily. Her hands fell away to lie on the bed--she was on her way to climax, and outwardly helpless. As he continued to suck up and down on her tongue, her gasps and moans increased in frequency. Her entire body was a field of tiny quivers. He did not need to move much in his awkward position, for she had muscles inside that acted like strong massaging hands around his member. At the height of her fervor, her limbs jerked slightly, and her entire body quivered. Jory rose toward climax about the same time, and they cried out together, squeezed each other, thrashed, and finally collapsed in a spent tangle of limbs.

"What have we done?" she whispered thickly, the bluish tip of her tongue still visible.

"We've done something we shouldn't," Jory whispered. He kissed her lips, and she thrust the tip of her still firm tongue between his lips. "But I truly love you," he added.

"And I love you, my darling. You are the only one who really loves me, and I love you."

"We can't do it again," Jory said, wanting to make love a thousand times that night for there must not be a second time.

"No, we cannot. But the laws are wrong. You are no more a--" (she couldn't say the word to his face) "--than I am. You have a soul, don't you? When you die, don't you go to Mount Oba and stand in the glowing fog?"

"Yes, my lady, my love. And we will stand together."

"You suggest--duello?" She asked the question with feigned casualness.

He laughed despite the grimness of their situation. "No, you silly one. I mean when we are old and die, we will be able to love each other forever where nobody can reach us."

"Maybe we'll run away," she thought, and immediately contradicted that thought. "No, because I would die without my baba."

It was true, Jory thought. That was the part of her culture he could never understand, not even after living with them for kjirs. The female and her birth sister, or baba, shared an entirely separate sexual liaison through which the male's seed was mixed with the female's, gestated inside the baba, and borne by her. The female was the child's seed mother, while the baba was its birth mother. Female and baba actually shared entirely different sex organs than those with which the female and the male communed. Without the love of her sister, Ramy would whither and die. He could not take her from here--the mere thought was ludicrous. So was the thought of maintaining this affair.

Jory and Ramy spent the next several days in a delirious half-life, much like the trance-like existence under the blanket. Each night, he stole to her bed and they passionately made love--real love, they both believed, not like the proprietary and violent seed-scattering performed by her husband before he returned to his skilled and inexhaustible concubines at Castle Dumonhi, or to his battles.

They were the most passionate nights of Jory's life. He would always carry with him his memories of lost treasure--the pleasure of entering her, the pleasure of taking her tongue in his mouth and feeling the quivers fly through her body while he pressed his weight on her and she held him tightly down, welcoming the pressure. When he did it pushup style, with his legs stretched straight behind, she would wrap her pale, smooth legs around his and squeeze. Her inner wet, smooth gripping muscles would massage him wildly, while her legs imprisoned him. It was a courtly love, full of tiny battles, conquests, taking of prisoners, sharing of captivity-- but the baba saw them one night.

They were finished in bed, and walked to the window to look over the night. The Obayyo glowed far away. It was a clear night, and the oaty, musky, sweet tywix was in full bloom so that the hills around the castle not only were fragrant, but glowed faintly.

Ramy had a bottle of last kjir's tywix wine, and she poured them each half a glassful. The glasses were round, open on top, and lay in the palm like a ball. In each glass she had dropped a candle wick that burned for a few minutes before going out. They each held a flickering ball of light representing the true love they felt for one another. For a seeming eternity they walked slowly, nakedly, arms around each other, to the window, while holding their glowing tywix balls close.

The spell was shattered when axes and swords ripped through the door. Shurian warriors poured in yelling and pointing. Right behind them were buzzing, angry babas with biolume torches pointing at the couple. No use trying to cover their nakedness. In her shame, Ramy tore from Jory's grasp and ran for the bed, to cover herself with a sheet. There, already, Jory glimpsed Ramy's baba holding the damp, love-soiled sheet up with a look of crazed triumph. Ramy regarded her sister with a dull shocked look of betrayal. She would have given her life for her sister. Jory tried to pull Ramy with him, but she screamed and ran to tear her baba's hair.

Jory grabbed what clothing he could and dove out the window. He ran as fast as he could, and several retainers after him. They had better night vision, but they appeared to be drunk. He knew the hidden paths and nooks better than anyone in the palace. He made his way to the Obayyo with only the clothes on his back. A million times, he would curse himself for not making a stand and dying with her. He could not imagine ever loving another person as much as he loved her, even though his love had cost her life...

Jory sat up in bed with a strangled cry. It had only been a dream. She was dead, lost, never to return. In the silence, it was as if she had never existed, the most cruel stroke of cold fate. He was soaked in sweat--not the warm secretions of love making, but the cold ocean water of deadly terror and unbearable loss.

One night, as Jory walked to his quarters after work, he thought he detected a familiar smell near the elevator shaft in his quiet corridor, but he could not place it. Later that night, as he lay studying astrogation and advanced mathematics, he received a vid from Aptath. He looked agitated. "We've got a situation, Jory. Need you down here right away."

Minutes later, with an escort, and still pulling his jumpsuit shut, Jory strode down the halls in Deck 38, a cargo deck near the ship's bottom. The smell was more noticeable now, and Jory could almost place it as he hurried along plain, utilitarian corridors with black steel floors and ceilings. Every two man-lengths a round biolume in mid-ceiling cast its island of cold light.

Captain Aptath met him at an intersection. He took Jory by the arm and roughly pulled him around a corner. "You are the only person who can possibly know what this means."

Storage unit doors made a line down the corridor. One door had bulged open, and a wheat-colored mass flowed out like dry foam. "Do you know anything about this? Is this some Oban deception?"

"Sir, I don't know what you are talking about."

Aptath grunted and let go. "Forgive me if I'm upset, but we seem to be losing part of our cargo here."

Jory brushed his arm off, and stumbled through the material. Now he recognized it, and he understood why the captain had called him--the smell was of tywix! "Is this a shipment from Oba? from Shur?"

"Damn right it is! Look what's inside."

Jory waded through the tywix foam, knee deep in places. The storage room was about twenty body-lengths to a side and ten lengths tall. Its walls were wood-paneled. This was delicate cargo--containers of fungi, some large, some small. Racks of small urns sat on pallets in a corner. Large aluminum containers were stacked to the ceiling against the back wall. Stacks of smaller containers were piled here and there--enough wealth here for a kingdom, Jory thought.

In the center of the mess stood a man in a biotech's white overalls. He was a tall, relatively slender Ruandap with a mussy mane, and he shook his head as he waved an instrument around. "Do you know anything of this?" the biotech asked Jory.

"No. I've never seen the tywix behave this way." Jory slogged toward him, Aptath and one or two security guards trailing. "My God." Shock overwhelmed Jory. He was staring into the face of a baba--or what was left of her. Slowly, he recognized her--Ramy-baba!

Somehow, instead of killing herself, the baba must have bribed cargo carriers to bring her to Kusi-O. But why? She must have killed Ramy to prevent any worse pain coming to her at Dumonhi hands. Then why did she not die with her? With all the clout the babas had, even in shady areas, this one had gotten herself smuggled away from the castle, perhaps among outlaws in the distant interior. But she'd stayed in the aluminum container. Most likely, as she had planned, she'd suffocated. For some reason, the tywix in her container had begun to froth up, as if it were sporing time. It had forced the container to split apart, and the fungus had kept increasing its size over and over until it filled the room and pushed the door out. Then it must have begun to die. By now only a million dry and lifeless tiny husks were left.

At Jory's feet, on the surface of the wheat-colored tywix, was a dark stain like a carelessly tossed blanket--her body. At one end was a smaller stain the size of a smashed melon--Jory recognized the baba's face.

"It is still alive," the biotech said waving his gadget. "But it is near death."

"She is a female," Jory said, "from my birth world. She is the sister of my mistress." He could not believe his great fortune--even

to see only the sister-baba of the woman he'd loved. "Ramy-baba,"
he whispered, afraid to touch her, for fear her desiccated body might
fall apart. There was almost nothing left of her--she'd become part of
the foam, and as her face slowly vanished, she would cease to be.
Why had she done this? "Ramy-baba," he repeated over and over.

Her eye slits trembled. Jory wondered if she could see him at
all. Her remaining shreds of skin looked black-brown like rotten
fruit atop the foam. Her mouth was a raw gash, part foam, part
rotting skin. Her nose was an indistinct feature passing no air. Her
last exhalation had left a tiny mound of brown foam by one nostril.
Now she breathed only shallow breaths with her mouth. As her inner
organs shut down and turned to foam one by one, that too would
cease.

"Why?" Jory asked. "Why?" He murmured: "Ramy-baba!"

Her mouth struggled to form a word: "Jory" or did she say
"Sorry?"

He gave the Shurian sign of forgiveness by touching two
fingertips to her cheeks. He felt a little bit of sharp bone under the
scrap of skin. "I love you," he told the baba. It was the first time he'd
ever said that to a baba.

Her eyes closed briefly in acknowledgment. "*Gyen.* Thank
you."

Then she opened her eyes, and, looking down, guided his gaze.
"Take," she croaked. All he could see was one hand, or what was
left of it, looking like shreds of a brown glove. She would never lift
that hand again. Maybe it wasn't even connected to her anymore.
"Your hand?" he asked.

She had no strength left. She closed her eyes in assent.

He poked warily, and the skin that had been her hand fell apart
in slimy flakes. He pushed the flakes aside, feeling something hard.
Poking some more, he felt a handle. He grasped it and pulled.

"It is dying," the biotech said, looking at his instrument rather
than at her.

Jory pulled out a duello short-sword. So Ramy had committed
suicide, and her sister had brought the other knife to Jory? Why? It
made no sense.

"It is gone," said the biotech. "Wait!"

Jory stared at the knife, created for birth and the mutual suicide of lovers. He blinked back tears. He recognized the Oban calligraphy on its handle.

As he read the poem, he smiled at a bitter-sweet memory.

He'd seen those very twin knives on a shelf in the Great Hall of Ramyon. In Oban warrior culture, such twins were the most favored gift given to lovers, reminding each of the blood bond of truth and life, and the succor of dying together in the final climax--dying in love, as they had loved in life.

The terrifying pact was sealed and softened with a most innocent of bed-time tales for small children, from the stories of Rabbit-in-the-Grass. The philosophical little rabbit who amused Oba children through the centuries was a funny little guy who observed all, understood nothing, yet survived and conveyed wisdom through his acceptance of truth.

As Jory read the inscription, he remembered what its mate must always say.

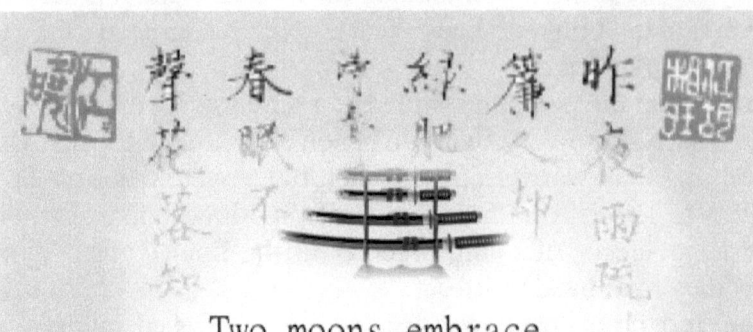

Two moons embrace
above the koh tree.

Celestial dome turns,
hiding moons behind
tree trunk.

Rabbit-in-the-Grass
catches his breath -
will reappear soon?

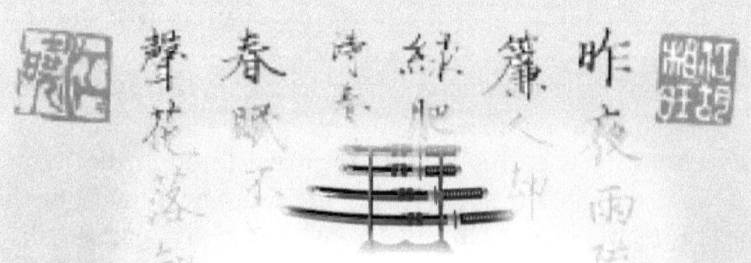

Celestial dome turns,
revealing what hid
behind the koh.

Not a single moon
in sight,
alas.

Rabbit-in-the-Grass
sighs and hops away.

The Biotech said: "Wait! Something else is alive under there. Something new that wasn't alive a minute ago."

Jory already half-understood. That spark...it had synapsed, a last gift from one love to another.

Jory carefully used his fingers to probe through the foam until he came to a rubbery surface. He dug the foam away with his hands, and the biotech helped. In places where body parts still hung together, Jory carved them apart.

Together, they exposed a long birth-sac--not the tiny birth-sac of a Shurian infant, but one large enough to hold a fully grown person.

"Easy," the biotech said. "There is a heart beating, but irregularly." He yelled: "Captain! we need to get this individual to the hospital immediately."

Jory rode in the ambulance to the Human Acute Clinic of Dora Mora's onboard hospital. With advice from encyclopedic expert systems, the ship's surgeons worked on the sac. Jory stood behind an observation window and watched the slow, careful cutting. He watched the flood of reddish-brown liquid into a drainage pan. A surgeon cut the thick membrane away while other techs applied oxygen and chest massage.

"It's alive," someone said. Jory slumped into a chair with relief.

Malinu excused Jory from work. Jory stayed as close as he could. They moved her to the intensive care unit, and Jory sat outside, sleeping or reading.

A doctor came out--a human doctor, an intelligent looking woman with yellow skin and high-cornered eyes. "I'm Doctor Pren. How are you?" They shook hands. "Is she a relative of yours?"

Jory almost laughed. "What do you mean?" He'd almost blurted that she was an alien.

"She asked for two persons--you, and someone named Baba."

Jory explained: "They are trisexual. There's a male, a female, and a baba..."

"Sir, what are you talking about? That is a human being in there, same as you and I."

"What?"

Dr. Pren put a finger over her lips. "Sh! Come and peek, only for a minute."

Jory followed her into the sick bay, where instruments flowed on the walls, monitors hummed, and intravenous fluids dripped above a sterile white bed. On the bed lay a naked human woman. Instead of a russet ball of fuzz, she had thickly flowing red hair that glowed like wet copper. She had horn-like plates like his own, Jory saw with a sinking feeling--but, to his relief, much smaller than his. They would not detract from her beauty--actually, they seemed to add something that Nolani's had not added. Ramy's skin was no longer transparent, but palest coffee. Her slender and lovely body bore galaxies of orange freckles. She was hooked up with tubes at every orifice, and wires ran to skin patches over much of her torso and on the major arteries of her limbs. A net-cap robot performed an ongoing brain scan. She had small, firm breasts, a bushy Venus-mound covered with orange curls, and a distinctly human kjoni. Jory looked closely at her fingertips-- the fingernails were like his own.

And yet, standing back, he recognized her exact form as that of Ramy.

"Is she--?"

"She is perfectly normal," Dr. Pren said. "I've never actually seen anything like it. She's newborn, but has mature brain wave function. What was that entity who gave birth to her?"

Jory explained about life on Oba Island and about the babas. Someone brought kjaba and Jory welcomed its warmth and bitter taste.

Dr. Pren took a speculative breath and nodded slowly as she ushered Jory out of the room. They spoke outside in the waiting room. Jory explained about their love affair.

"My guess," said Dr. Pren, "is that she will enjoy full human body and brain function. She asked for people by name--that's a sure sign. One thing puzzles me. These babas may be natural wizards of fungi and genetics and finance back there on Shur, but there is no way the baba could have obtained genes for the female from you.

You see, the female genetic material can only come from a human woman's egg. And there was no human female involved."

"Oh yes there was." Jory put his hands over his face in horror, remembering Xinda. What else had they taken from the child before blinding her and thrusting her into the night into the arms of her terrified parents? "The babas collect things, Doctor. They have thousands of kjirs of baba-craft behind them. Who knows how many human females they collected eggs from, who knows for what purpose?"

Ramy woke a few days later. Jory stayed outside for the first few hours while Ramy was taken to Human Less Acute, where human nurses fussed over her. They had not told her about her sister's death, or about Jory. Ramy was still on I.V. fluids, and very confused, but she received her first cup of citrus juice.

Dr. Pern met Jory in the hall. "Our young lady is doing fine. Now would be a good time to gently appear and take her hand. We'll monitor her respiration and other vital signs."

Jory stepped inside. Ramy did not see him yet. He heard her speak in Oban, asking for her sister. She sounded dazed.

Jory rounded the corner and stood before her bed. Ramy seemed not to recognize him. She wore a plain white smock that barely covered her torso. She was Ramy in a human incarnation--her sister's immense gift of atonement.

Ramy stared at Jory and her face betrayed a distant recognition, a horror. She reached up with both hands and touched the astropath plates. She made an unpleasant face. She reached anxiously around the side of her neck, on both sides, looking for the sex organs that weren't there any more. She must have realized the full story just then, for she let out a long wail of grief that rose up and down like a siren, like an animal keening for the loss of its mate. People held their ears. She threw herself on her back, then on her front, pounding the bed with her fists. A Ruandap doctor came running, as did a Fril nurse and human nurses. Dr. Pern stepped in with a look of concern, of speculation, weighing one plan against another.

"Leave her alone," Jory told them all. "She is grieving for her sister. There is nothing we can do until she is ready to receive our comfort."

Ramy screamed and threw herself on her back. She felt her mouth with both hands. She stuck her fingers in her mouth and screamed again--hoarse, anguished screams of rage and denial-- she'd died in her natural body, and now awakened as an alien. She grew silent with shock as she probed her belly with both hands, looking for the male-taking hole that wasn't there. Her fingers didn't dally over her new navel, for Shurians had that too.

Then she discovered that, before everyone, she'd let her new bladder and her bowels go, and she held up her hands which were smeared with blood and feces. She swayed from side to side, uttering a distressed animal's groaning.

Dr. Pern clapped a curtain shut, cutting Jory out. "She wouldn't want you to see her like this." She added: "Not the scene we'd hoped for, is it? But she's alive, and she's got normal function. And she has spoken. I suspect she is in total shock, and it will take time. Will you work with us?"

"Of course."

Jory went to see Captain Aptath and said: "Captain, we must ensure that the baba's remains are enurned to give to her sister.

Aptath bowed slightly and whispered a Ruandap saying of respect: "You always show us the honorable way."

Ramy-baba's remains were gathered, cremated, and sealed into an Oban-style burial tube with dark blue calligraphy on a cream-colored background. Jory took the burial tube to the hospital. Ramy tearfully accepted the tube, thanked him, and placed it by her pillow. She wore a plain, rumpled hospital gown, and pushed an intravenous diffusion pole as she walked slowly, but the mouth and nose tubes were gone, and she could eat nearly solid food now. "My organs are new, and they are helping me to train myself. I have to get used to this person I now am. I am human." She wrapped her free arm through his. She glanced at the burial tube. "That is all I have left of who I was, and of her. She was the love of my life."

"I know she was."

"Can you accept who I was?"

"I accepted you then, when we were willing to die for each other."

"I was right about you." She embraced him and rested her cheek against his chest. "I can hear your heart beating. I used to listen to it after you fell asleep, when we were children."

"I never knew that."

She grinned. "You didn't have to know everything."

They kissed, rubbing the tips of their tongues together in circles. They broke up laughing. "Not the same, is it?" she said.

"It will serve us."

The very next day, she was released from the hospital. Jory took her home, and she set up her nest as any human woman would, putting this here and that there, standing back, shaking her head, and reversing where the things sat. They made love in the human manner. Soon, she would begin training as an astropath. Aptath wrung his hands in delight every day. Malinu cast covetous glances, but he saw from Ramy's expression she would share herself with nobody but Jory. Malinu needed to glance at Jory only once.

The day came when Jory explained the nature of their gift, and she touched her own keradz with a mix of annoyance and awe. Jory took her to their place of work. She gasped as they entered the small theater where the ship's astropath chairs stood in a row under a huge glass bubble beyond which stretched the eternity of the universe.

As she stared into space, her eyes wide at the sight of so many stars, so many swirling galaxies, she cried out: "The Obayyo!"

He looked at fields upon fields of stars. For a moment he digested her confusion, then reached his arm around her. "Yes, a Lantern Road. It will be good to travel." He squeezed her close to him and added: "Together."

(back to top)

More Info: Worlds of John Argo

John Argo is a writer of Science Fiction, Dark Fantasy, and Science-Horror Fiction (SH, or Dark SF). He lives with his wife and family in Southern California.

Whenever you read a John Argo story or novel, no matter how dark or thrilling, you will usually also find a love story. In these tales, we travel to the far sectors of the human existence, while the characters' search for meaning glows like a lantern in darkness. Trust John Argo as a frequent traveler and tour guide along highways through imaginative space and time.

John Argo's web presence is at Clocktower Books (world's first real digital publisher*, online since 1996):

www.clocktowerbooks.com

The Internet information includes a complete list of the author's works and a detailed history of the Empire of Time.

Clocktower Books

*Clocktower Books was, to our knowledge, the world's first publisher to ever publish real digital (HTML), proprietary (not public domain), novel-length fiction (standard book length) online in digital format for reading in HTML online (not on portable media, e.g. CD-ROM). We also offered a TXT download.

We launched this program in early 1996, using an innovative process of publishing weekly serial chapters. Readers who needed to know the outcome, and couldn't stand the suspense, could email for a complete digital text file anywhere in the world. We received raves and kudos from around the globe. We used this serial chapter method to publish three John Argo books over 1996-1996: This Shoal of Space and Pioneers (both SF); and Neon Blue, a suspense novel. All three novels were bestsellers in the earliest e-book forums, including the original Barnes & Noble website in 2000, and other venues including Rocket eBooks.

Publisher's Dedication

(Circa 2007:) To **Deep Outside SFFH**, the world's oldest professional web-only magazine of science fiction, fantasy, and horror (speculative & dark fiction), launched April 15, 1998 by Brian Callahan and John T. Cullen. An archive site is still maintained (www.deepoutside.com). Small but mighty, the magazine was and is an innovator stressing quality over quantity, equally valuing literary and commercial components of short fiction, promoting the particular strengths of digital media without losing what has been great about print media.

The magazine continued uninterruptedly publishing online as **Far Sector SFFH** (www.farsector.com/) until January 2007 under the sole proprietorship of John T. Cullen, with help from a team of dedicated volunteer authors and editors (see below and website). Far Sector SFFH has an entry at the online SF Encyclopedia, while Deep Outside SFFH will be featured in Mike Ashley's fourth in a quartet of scholarly books on the history of SF magazines (Liverpool University Press). (Note 2015: look for Wikipedia entries soon, long overdue.)

Strengths include new modes of distribution that break from the past and work with innovators like Fictionwise (fictionwise.com) (2015 Note: sadly, Fictionwise was killed off 2012 by B&N).

Deep Outside SFFH (originally Outside: Speculative & Dark Fiction) became the first web-only professional magazine listed in Writer's Market (1999 Edition) alongside the pulps.

Founders were John T. Cullen and Brian Callahan. Significant contributors have been A. L. Sirois, John Kenneth Muir, Dennis Latham, and Shaun Farrell, plus of course all the authors we published over a decade. We published many unknown newcomers, as well as established talent. Some of these authors already had won prestigious awards (Pat York, Nebula), while others went on from obscurity to win important awards and nominations (Tim Pratt, Ted Kosmatka, Kameron Hurley, and many others).

Most important, of course, is content. While digital innovations are exciting, there is no substitute for good old-fashioned storytelling from fine authors like Dennis Latham, Pat York, Melanie Tem, Joe Murphy, A. L. Sirois, Joel Best, and many others the magazine has sent to your viewing surface.

Message sent back in time to the Futurians of the 1930s: *"We have landed in the future, which we find to be exhilarating. Maybe 'breathtaking' and 'terrifying' would be better adjectives. Humans are still behaving stupidly, and wantonly killing each other, so we add 'disappointing.' Will send full report soon. Aim your crystal radio sets to the following coordinates..."*

About the Empire of Time Series

This novel is one of several novels slated for the Up Time Sector of John Argo's vast, sprawling future history series **Empire of Time.**

A longer history of the Empire of Time series and its Sectors, has been moved to the website www.clocktowerbooks.com or to an appropriate venue (e.g. www.empireoftime.com TBD).

A more complete chronology, synopsis, and other information can be found on line at Clocktower Books.

You can always be sure of two things: (1) original and compelling stories and (2) fascinating and engaging heroes and heroines (often with a strong romantic subplot).

The following generic Empire of Time image is adapted from an older cover image for *Pioneers* (Side Time Sector) by John Argo (also available for your reading pleasure at major retailers).

Empire of Time

Blue Barbarian Princess Auska amid star port ruins on N60A
(from *Pioneers*)

SF Series by John Argo

www.ingramcontent.com/pod-product-compliance
Lightning Source LLC
Chambersburg PA
CBHW020617130626
46552CB00003B/1015